WE THUGGIN': SAINT & SINNA'S STORY

TAYLOR B

TAYLOR'S INK PRESENTS

After battling one hardship after another Sinna Fletcher goes from a chaotic life with a drug-addicted mother to trying to prevent her older sister from going down the same path. Her sister, Simone takes advantage of Sinna's generous and loving nature leaving Sinna standing alone to pick up the pieces in the wake of her decisions. A last-ditch effort to keep her head above water puts her in the crosshairs of the unpredictable and untrusting X'keem "Saint" Daniels.

Saint loves the attention he attracts from women, he's a lover and he's not afraid to share himself with whatever woman he chooses, much to his girlfriend's displeasure. Life hardened his heart robbing any woman a chance at really obtaining it. He loves that Sinna's a little rough around the edges and before either of them realizes it their lives are entangled and spiraling out of control.

He's a self-admitted sinner and she's far from a saint herself, will these two be able to come to a middle ground to make their love affair work? Follow these two in We Thuggin' to find out!

1

SINNA

"Excuse me, ma'am, can I check your bags please?" the ro-bo cop asked as he stopped me from leaving.

Well, he didn't really stop me from leaving I could have outrun his ass if I wanted to, well, maybe if I didn't have a baby and a stroller full of stolen shit. The loud ass alarm system alerted him that I was walking out the store with merchandise that was tagged with an anti-theft tag.

"Sure," I lied.

Right on cue, Justyce started crying when the security guard took the bracelet out his tiny fingers.

"Oh, he must have grabbed it when we were at the register," I lied looking at Justyce with a fake scowl on my face.

It was the same face I gave him when we played, so he laughed his usual laugh making both me and the security guard erupt in laughter as well.

"It's alright ma'am, I have a baby at home. I completely understand," the security guard said adding a smile while touching Justyce's hand.

"Thank you, Sir. Have a good day!" I said with a smile as we walked out of the store and out to the parking lot where my sister, Simone was waiting in our crackhead rental.

I loaded the car up with the bags from the store, pulled a pair of jeans from under my clothes, and put Justyce in the car seat without her help. It wasn't until I was loading the stroller in the rusty trunk that I realized Simone didn't even bother to help get her son buckled into the car seat and opted instead to make gun fingers as she performed to the song on the radio.

"You straight?" she asked as we pulled out of the parking lot.

I rubbed my fingers together quickly, rocking left and right in my seat focused on warming up before I spoke.

"I'm gone be great once we sell all this shit," I said as I blew hot air against my cold, tingling fingertips.

The small amount of heat the older model car was putting out felt more like air conditioning by the time it hit my face.

"You got everything?" Simone asked with wide eyes.

"Yup, I got the shit that was on the list and then some," I grinned.

"Good, cause I'm fucking hungry," Simone whined rubbing her pudgy stomach.

"Simone, all we got is two dollars and that gotta go in the tank so we can get across town," I reminded her as she passed by a gas station.

"Look, I'm hungry now," she blew me off.

See, this was the shit that kept me frustrated with her. All she had to do was wait until we could get these orders out and we would be straight. But no, this bitch is hungry, so instead of putting gas in the bullshit ass ride we had, she would rather fill her stomach. I couldn't believe she was pulling into McDonald's, but what took the cake was when this bitch parked and got out to get her food. I shook my head as I watched her inhale half of our gas money not once turning around to feed her hungry son. I shook my head at her antics and blew out the breath I was holding, in an effort to calm down.

When we finally pulled into a gas station I jumped out with the dollar in my hand. I had to get away from my sister before I hurt her. A few steps ahead of me sat two shiny quarters.

"Thank you, mama," I whispered after I picked them up.

Thanking my mama for looking out for me was something I started doing after she died. I didn't know if she was actually helping me cause it was no doubt in my mind that Ana Jackson busted hell wide open. Maybe it was my absent father, I don't know but somebody was looking out for a bitch and I was thankful as hell.

"Oh, shit excuse me," I said bumping into someone as I opened the door and walked in.

"You good Shorty. I should have been paying better attention," he said with a smile.

This nigga was fine as FUCK! He was way taller than me with a peanut butter skin tone, pretty ass brown eyes, and long-ass dreads all poured into a sexy ass body that had Ms. Kitty in full throttle. He was wearing a white, green, and red collar shirt with acid wash jeans and shoes I couldn't pronounce or afford. Even if he was standing in front of me wearing nothing but the long Jesus piece around his neck and the two nice ass rings on his fingers he was still out of my damn league. Shit, I was trying to get enough gas in the piece of shit hooptie I borrowed from a crackhead, so we could make some money to last us until Saturday when Simone went back to work.

"You good lil mama?" he asked as I stood there frozen like a motherfucka.

"Uhh yeah, I'm good," I said brushing past him to stand behind the only person in line to put $1.50 in the gas tank.

"Hey, can I get this on pump six?" I said sliding the money across the counter to the cashier.

"Will that be regular or..."

"Regular," I said slightly rolling my eyes.

Regular gas was two dollars and thirty-seven cents, why would I be putting premium in the motherfucka? I couldn't help but feel like the bitch behind the glass was trying to be funny, but I didn't have time to care about her bullshit, I had business to handle. I wasn't going to cause a scene, but I did send a mug her way as I back peddled towards the door and walked right into a hard body.

"Damn," I said looking up into the sexy stranger's face.

"Where you going, with just a dollar and change ma?" he asked now crossing his tattooed covered arms in front of me.

First, it was the cashier trying to be funny about the dollar and fifty cents I was putting in the car, and nowhere this pretty motherfucka was standing in my face giving me the same face.

"First of all, yo ass listening way too damn hard and it ain't none of your business! I gotta go!" I said trying to get past him.

"Yo, you got a slick mouth. I was just trying to help yo ass, but fuck it, I hope that raggedy motherfucka break down stupid ass bitch," he said and then he walked over to the register completely ignoring me.

"Fuck you too! That's why yo breath smell like dog shit!" I lied as I stormed out of the store.

I walked out the door and over to the car to put the gas into the tank. As soon as I pumped the gas I got in and slammed the door closed.

"What's wrong with you?" she asked glancing at me.

She didn't even wait for me to respond before she was back paying more attention to the phone in her hand than anything else. The glass doors of the store opened and the sexy ass nigga with the foul mouth walked his bow-legged ass out the store. He refused to look over at me while I mugged as him hard as I could.

"Simone let's go," I urged my sister.

"Chill bitch, I'm trying to get my sugar daddy to cash app me something," she said rolling her eyes.

Finally, a few seconds later she started the car and we pulled off. We turned left on Glenwood Avenue, only for the raggedy piece of shit we were driving cut off in the middle of the busy street.

"What the fuck?" Simone asked trying to start the car again.

It started, rumbled for a few seconds allowing her to maneuver it over a little to the shoulder and then cut off again.

"Fuck!" she yelled hitting the steering wheel.

"I told you we should have used all the money for gas," I spoke lowly shaking my head.

"Look, I gotta feed my baby!" she snapped at me with tears in her eyes.

"BABY?" I yelled looking at her in disbelief.

As if our situation wasn't bad enough, this bitch was adding fuel to an already out of control forest fire. Simone and I had to move into my aunt's two-bedroom apartment about six months ago because Simone stopping paying the bills in our apartment in anticipation of getting money from our mom's life insurance policy. Turns out, when you commit suicide your life insurance doesn't have to pay your family.

Who knew?

I didn't know, but I did plead with her to continue paying the bills, but she refused. She could have paid a few bills with as much money as she was making as a stripper, but she spent it on clothes and partying instead. I guess our mini argument was doing too much for Justyce cause he started crying which got under Simone's skin.

"God, I wish he would just shut the fuck up!" she yelled hitting the steering wheel making the horn go off.

"I can't believe you, Simone! We struggling to make it and you go and get pregnant. You know Red ain't gone let you strip if you pregnant, especially after you were just fighting in the club," I told her referring to the owner of the strip club.

Part of the reason we were in the situation we were in was due to her getting into a fight with another stripper over her ain't shit baby daddy, Dirty. The nigga was constantly begging her for money, fucking his other baby mamas and future baby mamas. But she loved him to no end.

"Maybe I don't want to be a fucking stripper! You ever thought about that shit? Why don't you go strip?" she asked unbuckling her seatbelt.

"You know what? *If* I was irresponsible enough to not pay my fucking bills, I would do whatever to take care of my son and to help take care of my younger sister, selfish ass bitch!" I told her.

I was so fucking angry I could have snapped her neck like a fucking pencil. Just as I was getting ready to really tell her how I felt, somebody knocked on the passenger side window. I looked up to see the handsome stranger from the store standing there.

"Y'all good?" he asked through the glass.

He looked in the backseat at a crying Justyce and then back at me before his eyes traveled over to Simone.

"No, we good, we'll figure it out." I spoke up dismissing him.

"Nah, we need some help. You think you can give us a ride to Spring Forest Rd?" Simone asked him, leaning over batting her eyelashes at dude.

I sat back against the worn, dusty seats pushing my lips into a strong pout as I crossed my arms across my chest.

"Yeah, I can help y'all out," he said smirking at me.

He opened my door for me and the cold air smacked me in the face. I opened the back door handed the handsome strangers all eight bags from Macy and then grabbed Justyce. My eyes drifted over to the Hot Wheels decorated Tahoe with the custom money green paint and huge chrome rims. I watched Simone's hoe ass slid in the passenger side, not bothering to help with her son or his car seat. I pulled Justyce's car seat from the car and dude from the store took it out my hands.

"I'm Saint by the way," his smooth voice lured my attention from the dick print my eyes were now focused on.

"Your real name is Saint?" I asked in disbelief as I studied his body.

"Why?" he frowned.

"You're Saint and I'm Sinna," I explained.

The laugh that rolled out of him sent chills through me, or maybe it was twenty-degree North Carolina weather, either way, this nigga had my attention. Justyce laughed along with him on my hip grabbing my attention.

"That's funny lil man?" Saint asked as he tickled Justyce.

"I'm sorry about—wait a minute. No, I'm not, you called me a bitch," I said, propping my hand on my hips.

"My fault shorty. " he offered.

The nonchalant apology rolled off his lips easily. His apology wasn't heartfelt and judging by the way his eyes kept roaming over my body he liked what he saw. I didn't want to get in the truck with him, but I needed a ride, Simone was already in the car, and if nothing else, he would be a good distraction from the bullshit that was my life.

"Come on, let's get little man out the cold," he told me, ushering me over to his truck.

Saint opened the back door on the driver's side door for me and sat the car seat on the leather seat. I stood Justyce up inside the truck in front of the seat while I struggled to buckle his car seat in.

"Let me help you shorty, pass me lil man," Saint said reaching for Justyce.

He rubbed his dick against my ass as he reached for Justice who didn't complain about the stranger reaching for him. Shit, I wasn't complaining about Saint standing behind me either. I could tell he hadn't initiated contact with me on some creep shit, but now that our bodies were touching, he wasn't pulling away either. Once I got his car seat in and I was sitting inside the car with the car seat in the middle seat and me on the outside, he handed Justyce back to me.

"Thank you," I said glancing at him again.

"Wassup? I'm Kidd," the nigga sitting on the other side of Justyce spoke to me.

Damn, what my mama always said was true; *birds of a feather flocked together*, cause this nigga here could get it too. I could tell by the way his long legs were positioned he was tall, he wasn't as muscular as Saint, but his smooth, pretty boy baby face went along with his nickname very well.

"Sinna," I offered a small smile to him.

"Aight, so y'all gone have to give us directions." Saint said glancing at me in the rearview mirror.

"Oh, where y'all from?" Simone asked as her eyes lit up.

I swear I loved my sister, but her hoe ass was sitting there with one baby on my hip and another in her belly, yet she had the nerve to be flirting with these niggas. Okay, maybe I was just tight cause she was directing her hoe talk towards Saint.

"Them thick ass accents, I can tell y'all from somewhere deep in the south," she said rubbing Saint's arm.

I felt Saint's eyes dart to me in the rearview mirror before he glanced back over at Simone.

"We grew up in Atlanta." Kidd told us.

"Okay, ATL shawty," Simone danced in her seat playfully.

I pushed my back further into the seat and glanced out the window in an attempt to disappear.

God, please let this ride go by fast, I thought.

Simone kept the boys entertained while she gave directions. I kept my mouth shut and watched life happen outside my window while Justyce bobbed his head to the Jay-Z that poured through the speakers.

"Yo, lil man cool as hell. Who got him listening to Hov?" Saint asked with a huge smile as he turned the volume down.

Why he gotta be so fine?

"We both listen to Hov, he the goat, fuck you mean?" Simone asked irritating the shit out of me.

For some people, traumatic events changed them, but not Simone. She'd always been self-centered and manipulative, so I guess it was me that changed. Her behavior bothered me, but we were always a unified front when it came to our mother, so her behavior didn't bother me as bad, I guess. Now, she was quickly joining the list of people I didn't want around me. Before I turned eighteen, I depended on Simone to pay bills, buy food, typical grown people shit and then my mom died, and we quickly spiraled out of control. Don't get it twisted, my mom wasn't *a mom* to me. She lived with us on paper, but we'd put her out a long time ago. She had no boundaries, nothing was off-limits when she needed a hit, it was almost like she didn't care that she was hurting us. She had to feed her daily growing habit by any means necessary, even if that meant being a neglectful mother to her kids.

"I ain't trying to be all in yo business or nothing like that, but how y'all out shopping at Macy's and H & M and shit when you driving a 30-year-old car?" Saint asked.

"Does it matter?" I asked with a raised eyebrow staring into his eyes through the mirror.

"Aye, we ain't have to stop and help y'all, we can drop y'all off right here," Kidd spat, speaking up while he eyed me.

"Chill," Saint said glancing at him and then back at me.

"We had to get out there and get it. Them people ain't gone miss the little bit of shit we stole," Simone replied, confirming what I'm sure Saint was getting at.

I shot Simone a look ready to go off on her, but her simple ass wasn't paying me any fucking attention. She knew better than to be telling my business and yeah, she might have been stripping, but it was me out here stealing shit, not *us* as she liked to say.

"What would have happened if you got caught stealing them people shit?" Saint asked still focused on me.

I didn't have a choice, it wasn't just me I was sticking my neck out there for. If I didn't go out and do shit like this, who would?

"Yo y'all thieving' asses gotta get the fuck on," Saint replied when I didn't answer him.

The truck rolled to a complete stop, he popped the locks and locked eyes with me in the rearview mirror.

"Let's talk about this," Simone voiced her opinion.

"Simone, the nigga said he wanted us out. Ain't shit left to say," I said unbuckling my seat belt preparing to get out of the truck.

"Damn, shorty got a pair," Kidd busted out laughing along with Saint a second later.

"I'm just fucking with you," Saint said putting the truck back in drive.

Before I could respond, a car came to a screeching halt stopping in front of us, preventing us from moving forward. The front doors flew open and two females jumped out the car and headed in our direction. Both girls had video vixen bodies and long bundles that bounced off the fur coats they wore as they approached the truck.

"Damn," Saint groaned.

The first girl pulled the door handle and snatched the truck door open, stuck her head inside and looked around before she mushed Saint in the head.

"What the fuck is going on in here?" she yelled mushing Saint in the head two more times.

"What you doing yo?" Saint asked leaning back pushing her long-manicured nails out his face.

"This the bitch you cheating on me with Saint?" she asked.

"Erica, I'm just dropping them off," he replied.

"For real doe," Kidd spoke up.

"Shut yo lying ass up!" she barked at Kidd, who busted out laughing in response.

"You just a regular captain save-a-hoe, huh?" she asked with slanted eyes.

"Look, he really was just giving us a ride," I spoke up, hoping to move things along.

"Oh, now you got these bitches feeling comfortable enough to talk to me? This bitch got a baby in the backseat, you playing step daddy too?" the girl asked narrowing her eyes even more at Saint.

"Fuck you bitch! My son got a daddy!" Simone exploded as she tried to reach over Saint to get to her.

While they were fussing the back door opened and the other female reached in the truck and snatched the lace front ponytail wig, I was using for a disguise off my head. I didn't know this chick from a can of paint, so she was undeserving of an ass whooping or at least she was before she put her hands on me. And as angry as I was with Simone, I had more than enough ass whooping to go around.

X'KEEM A.K.A SAINT

X'KEEM A.K.A SAINT

One minute I was joking with the pretty ass girl in the back-seat of my truck and the next it was like a WWE street match out this bitch.

"Let go!" I boomed pulling Sinna's hands-off Jasmine's hair.

Sinna had Jasmine in a headlock and even with my body in between them as I tried to pull them apart, she held on to her tight grip. Sinna's dreads were pulled back into a ponytail that hung loosely off the side of her head while her and Jasmine continued going back and forth. Seeing Sinna's Cinnamon brown locs run across my knuckles forced me to take a second look at her that held me in place until Erica spoke again.

"You taking up for that bitch?" Erica screamed like her words were some sort of war cry before she dove on my ass.

I had no choice, but to let Sinna go and hold Erica off before I lost it and beat her ass myself.

"Stop fucking hitting me!" I barked.

"You always doing this shit!" she sobbed.

"I AIN'T DOING SHIT!"

"You ain't shit!" she said as tears rolled down her face.

"Yo, you blowing the fuck outta me right now! I ain't doing shit but taking them the fuck home!" I explained.

"Girl don't believe that nigga, he probably brought all them bags of shit from Macy's," Jasmine huffed now that Sinna had let her go.

"Why can't you love me as much as I love you?" she asked pushing me away with two hands.

"Erica, I ain't about to go back and forth with—" I told her trying to hold her hands.

We tussled over her manicured hands for a second or two before she snatched them away from me and took a step back.

"How many times am I going to look the other way while you fuck other bitches?" she asked wiping her face angrily.

"You ain't gotta look the other way. I told you I ain't fucking shorty, I just met her ass," I spat.

"I wish I never met you," she whispered as she backed away.

"Fuck," I groaned lowly as I watched her walk away.

I turned around to see Sinna climbing back in the truck and Simone letting Kidd look her over for injuries, I guess.

The rest of the four-minute ride to their house was quiet except for the constant vibrating of my cell phone. I didn't understand what the point of calling me back to back was after the shit that just happened, but this was typical Erica behavior. Fuss, fight, makeup, repeat, that was the seemingly never-ending cycle we'd been locked in over the past year. I can admit that most of the shit we went through was my fault, but I was really getting sick of the merry go round.

I ain't gone front, in the beginning, Erica could get damn near anything out of me. I was buying clothes and shoes, sending flowers to her house and shit, paying her bills and all. But it seemed like nothing I did was enough for her, the more

I did for her, the more she wanted until I didn't want to give her a dime.

"You can stop right here," Sinna said softly from the back seat.

I glanced at her in the rearview mirror, watching the little boy in the car seat play with her dreads. Before when I thought that was her hair swooped back in a ponytail, she was pretty, but now I couldn't keep my eyes off her. I had a thing for women with dreads for some reason. I knew Erica was going next level crazy because of Sinna's dreads. It seemed like all the bitches I'd cheated with had dreads or natural hair. I don't know what it was about natural hair that kept my attention, but if a bitch with dreads or braids wanted the dick, it was nothing anybody could do, I was fucking. I'd asked Erica on several occasions to go natural, shit it was in, it seemed like most bitches these days was doing it. For whatever reason, having natural hair was the only fad she wasn't interested in.

She'd been to the DR for the fat transfer and the breast implants and she stayed in the hair salon or the nail salon getting whatever Nikki Minaj, Cardi B, or whoever was popular at the time was getting done. I wasn't complaining cause whatever she did, she always looked good as hell, but it was her attitude that pushed me away. She was always bitching and complaining about some shit, nothing was ever good enough for her. No amount of money spent was enough for the shit she wanted. She felt since I was making fast money, she should be able to spend it just as fast. The only problem with that was, I wasn't dropping bands on her like she wanted me to. Erica worked as a bartender, she had a body and she was pretty as hell, so she made good money, but money ran through her fingers like water.

Kidd and I helped Sinna and Simone get all their bags, the car seat, and lil man to the front door. Simone wasted no time exchanging numbers with Kidd and then rushing in the house with the bags and the car seat leaving Sinna with lil man on her hip.

"Hold up shorty, let me talk to you for a second," I told her, grabbing her hand.

She snatched her hand away from me like it was on fire.

"What's up?" she asked.

"I just wanted to tell you, I'm sorry for that shit back there," I told her.

"Fuck you apologizing to me for?" she shrugged.

"I didn't want you to think that kind of shit usually happens around me." I explained.

She nodded her head slowly as she looked at me.

"Is that it?" she asked with a scowl.

I laughed at her expression, sending her turning around towards the house.

"Take care yo," I called out to her back.

She tossed two fingers up, chucking me the deuces without turning around as she walked into the house and closed the door behind her.

* * *

"I heard Erica turned into the incredible Hulk on yo ass," Khalifa said as soon as I walked in the trap.

"You gossip like a bitch yo," I turned around and grilled Kidd.

"Khalifa that shit was funny as fuck!" Kidd said laughing.

"He ain't have to tell me shit, Jasmine loud mouth-ass running around telling everybody." Khalifa said shaking his head.

"Fuck both of y'all. Y'all know she damn crazy. You should get yo girl man." I grilled him as I sat down on the raggedy couch.

"*My girl?* Nigga I been told yo ass all I give these bitches is dick. Nothing more." Khalifa schooled me.

"Everybody can't be out here pimping these hoes like you. On some real shit though, ain't shit wrong with fucking with one girl." Kidd replied sitting in the chair across from me.

"Shitting me," Khalifa laughed.

"Aight, y'all lil Kum By Ya moment is over, let's handle this business." I ushered them back to the business at hand.

Khalifa, Kidd, and I did a bunch of shit. We trapped, we robbed niggas, we did whatever we needed to do. My mama said I took after my daddy, but I ain't know the nigga and to be honest, she probably didn't either. I grew up constantly telling myself I ain't need a father, I had my Uncle David and my Aunt Nikki. Shit, I was good.

After working with Khalifa and Kidd the rest of the day we closed the trap and headed to drop off the money to this nigga named Corey. Corey was one of the niggas that Ace had working under him, I personally ain't like the nigga, but all we were doing was dropping off money and product and getting paid. Ace was my Uncle David's prodigy, Unc brought him into the game and as a favor to him he brought Khalifa, me and Kidd in. At first, Unc was pissed he wanted us to go to school and stay out the streets, but bills had to be paid and we needed to eat so we did what we had to do.

"What up?" Black asked.

Black looked more like a big ass black bear than a person, but he was good at his job. If the job was to stand in the way with a grimace to deter niggas from trying to run up in the spot. *The Spot* was a house Ace used to hold drugs and money. The only way a nigga was getting in, was if Corey wanted you to be there. Black and a slew of other beefed up niggas would give their lives to make sure of it.

"Sup. Corey know we coming," Khalifa spoke up.

"Bet." He nodded and opened the metal, steel door allowing us entrance.

We walked in past the first two rooms where five or six women stood in bikinis under clear raincoats as they cut and bagged powder. Another room was used for pills and weed with the same setup. We continued down the hall until we were met with another steel door with another big bear ass nigga with an AK strapped to his chest protecting it. He nodded at us and opened the door allowing us to walk past him. Inside the room long tables with small stacks of money in the center of them surrounded us. I glanced around the room but didn't focus on the money too long out of respect. Instead, I focused on this cartoon looking ass nigga that was walking towards us.

"What up fellas?" Corey asked coming towards us with a huge smile on his face.

"What up?" Khalifa nodded as he spoke.

Corey dapped up each of us and then took the duffle bag full of money and sat it in front of him while he ran it through a money counter.

"Damn, y'all grinding. I fuck with it." he complimented us with a head nod.

"Preciate it," Khalifa told him.

Corey knocked on the table with his fist three times and a chick wearing a tube top across her titties and a pair of boy shorts exposing her fat ass walked out from the back. She had a duffle bag strapped across her body that bounced against her with each step she took. She attempted to give it to Corey, but he shook his head and nodded towards Khalifa. She extended the duffle bag to Khalifa, he took it and nodded at Corey.

"Same time next week," Corey said dismissing us.

After splitting up the money amongst the three of us, I started to go home and deal with whatever drama Erica was brewing later but changed my mind after seeing the last book she'd sent through text. I knew from experience ignoring her temper tantrum would only piss her off more, so I hit a U-turn in the middle of the street and headed over to her house instead.

If I handled this situation right, I'd be able to bust a fat ass nut and go to sleep. I knocked on the door twice and rang the doorbell, but she didn't answer so I moved the mat and used the spare key to go into the house. I opened the front door to see every light on in the small two-bedroom apartment. I exhaled loudly dropping my keys in the candy dish on the table beside the door.

Erica was probably somewhere laid out in the floor half-drunk, half–high, half-sleep drooling on the floor. Pieces of clothing led a trail to the bedroom but seeing the big ass Jordan's just outside the door sent fire through my veins.

What the fuck?

I stood outside the bedroom door attempting to calm down before I removed my burner from behind my back and turned the doorknob stepping into the dark bedroom. My eyes adjusted to the darkness in the room as my brain recognized it was two bodies in her queen size bed. My eyes fluttered quickly as I tried to calm the adrenaline that rushed through my body.

"GET THE FUCK UP!" I yelled startling both Erica's dumb ass and whoever the old nigga lying beside her was.

"OH SHIT!" she yelled jumping her naked ass out of the bed.

"Yeah, oh shit." I repeated, keeping the forty-five-caliber gun at my waist instead of pointing it at them both and pulling the trigger.

"What the fuck? I swear—" the nigga with the salt and pepper goatee tried to explain himself.

"I don't want to hear shit you gotta say," I cut him off.

"Saint, please—"

"Please what? What? Don't shoot yo hoe ass?" I asked angrily.

"Aye, my man, she said she was single," the nigga said holding the blanket over his naked ass.

"I can't believe yo hoe ass tripping on me and you in here fucking a nigga! I ought to kill yo ass!" I barked.

"You gone kill me?" she asked, jumping up from her spot on the bed.

"Don't test me, Erica!" I told her, using the barrel of the gun to scratch my head.

"Shit, ain't fun when the rabbit got the gun?" Erica spat, putting on a tank top.

I nodded my head up and down and bit my bottom lip as I attempted to control my raging emotions. I knew I was supposed to count down when I got upset, but I was too angry to even remember what came next after ten.

"Niggas love to cheat and fuck bitches, but I do the same and it's an issue," she giggled as she shimmied into a pair of pajama pants.

I lifted the gun in my hand and fired a shot in Erica's direction.

"NIGGA YOU ALMOST SHOT ME!" she screamed in disbelief.

"And the next time I won't miss," I hissed. "Shit don't feel good do it?" I asked with a smile on my face.

"Y'all crazy as hell! Aye bro I'm sorry—"

I cut Granddaddy's words short when I fired a shot sending a bullet through his skull, sending him crashing to the floor.

"WHY WOULD YOU DO THAT?" Erica screamed hysterically.

"I ain't do that shit, YOU did that shit!" I exploded on her.

"He has kids—"

"I don't give a fuck about Big Ben's kids, fuck him and fuck you too bitch! I loved yo ass!" I spat.

"How? By fucking any bitch that came yo way? By not taking care of me?" she asked with a face soaked in tears.

"BY NOT FUCKING KILLING YOU RIGHT NOW!"

"If you kill me, then you're killing you cause I'm pregnant," she replied.

Silence filled the space between us as her words settled. Instead of responding I cocked the gun back and pointed it at her. She tucked her lips in her mouth and extended her hands to me.

"If you would just learn to trust a nigga then you would know today wasn't about me fucking with another bitch. I was only helping a fucking stranger out, but you just had to take things too fucking far. You actually brought a nigga here and fucked him!" I screamed.

"I'm pregnant." she sobbed.

"So, you fucked a nigga with my seed in you?" I questioned her.

"I'm sorry." She continued sobbing.

"Stay the fuck away from me or you will be," I told her.

"And what about our baby?" she asked.

"Get rid of it," I tossed over my shoulder without turning to face her.

I stormed out of the apartment before I lost the little bit of mind I had left before I killed her ass.

"Aye, I got some trash I need taken out at Erica's," I spoke into the phone once Khalifa answered.

"For her?" he asked.

"Nah, a guest," I replied.

"Sayless," he told me and hung up the phone.

2

SINNA

"Can I talk to you for a minute?" my aunt Trisha asked me.

I was sitting outside on the porch watching Justyce run and play while I tried to catch up on some GED homework. I should have graduated high school in May and then sign up for college with my friends over the summer.

But my mama died.

My life didn't change just because she died, but because of how Simone changed once she died. Simone was never the most organized or responsible person, but before our mom died, I could manage her and get her to do shit the right way, but now, she was out of control. We spoke, but anytime I brought up this baby situation she shut me out and refused to talk about it. She even stopped coming home after her shifts at the club. I loved my nephew, but she left me responsible for him without saying anything to me. It wasn't much of an adjustment since I cared for him most of the time anyway, but a heads up would have been nice.

"Yes, ma'am?"

"I'm not rushing y'all or nothing, but when y'all moved in, you said a couple of months and it's been close to four now," she replied, offering a sympathetic frown.

What did she want me to say? She knew first hand just how crazy life was for us right now. The past month almost I've had to borrow money from her to pay Justyce's daycare bill. Simone didn't send in her employment verification and social services were refusing to pay for his daycare until she did. Of course, when she was approved for food stamps and his daycare voucher, I made a fake paycheck stub that looked like my stub from my part-time job at Wendy's. I had the pay stubs ready and waiting for her whenever she decided to go turn the information in.

"I know Auntie, I'm trying to help Simone save money, so we can afford a down payment somewhere. It's just hard because I had to take some time off to focus on school, but I—"

"Sinna, you should be in high school, I know you feel like you gotta step in and help your sister, but Simone is twenty years old and if she doesn't fall on her ass and make some mistakes, she ain't gone ever learn," she said shaking her head.

"Auntie, I don't mind helping her out, I know it's hard being a single mom and—"

"Girl, if anything you the single parent! You bathe him, you feed him, you manage work, school and him. It's amazing that your so dedicated to making sure he's good, it reminds me of how your mom used to be, you know before the drugs. It's like you're her pre-drugs and Simone is how she was after. I love y'all, I really do, but Simone can't stay in my house, work and not pay bills. You ain't been working cause you taking off to watch him while she's out with his daddy probably making another damn child, she ain't gon take care of. It's not healthy and she don't respect my rules, every morning last week she had that nigga in my house." She said shaking her head.

So that's what all this was about. She was mad Simone was fucking Corey in her house and I guess I had an issue with that shit too cause me and her shared a queen-size bed and I ain't seen that bitch wash no damn sheets lately. Simone was used to doing whatever she wanted because my mom was always too high to really care or wasn't there because she was out somewhere trying to get high. Simone basically raised me, so how could I just turn and look the other way when she needed me?

"I'm sorry Auntie, I really am. I'll talk to her, I promise," I told her.

"That's the problem, she a grown-ass woman and she has no respect for anybody but herself. She does whatever the fuck she wants because she's holding onto the fact that you need somewhere to be, so I won't put you and Justyce out. I really want to look out for y'all the best way that I can since my sister didn't do that when she was alive and she damn sure can't do it now. I'm not kicking you out right now, but at tax time when she gets her tax money, y'all need to find something," she told me.

I had a little over two and a half months to find a place to stay. I couldn't work full time because I was focused on school, but I was passing so far, and I needed to focus on making money. I'd just take the test and pick up some fulltime hours. Then I'd be able to pay for all the extra hours of daycare for Justyce.

"Alright, Auntie," I agreed and focused my attention back on Justyce chasing birds in my Auntie's garden beside the house.

* * *

"Damn, Sinna you damn almost burnt the fries!" Money said, grabbing a carton of fries from the tray.

"I'm sorry I'm somewhere else right now." I told her

shaking my head.

I liked my job, meeting new people, interacting with people, especially when we stayed open late on weekends. Minyon or Money as we called her was one of my best friends. She was short, brown skin, with a big old bubble butt she swore every woman in her family had, and one of the most genuine people I've ever met.

"What's going on? I know you ain't tripping off AJ hoe ass?" Khadija asked.

Khadija was the final third of our little trio. She was funny and somewhat naïve, but over the past year, her and Money had become my best friends.

I'd been ignoring AJ's phone calls and text messages this weekend because he and his girlfriend both checked into a club in Miami on Facebook. They didn't check in together, but still the point is that he was supposed to be going to Miami for business, not to be caked up with the bitch he claimed he didn't want anything to do with. I didn't even have time to be worried or upset about that dumb shit. I liked AJ, he was cool and all, but he was a young boss nigga who was spoiled as fuck. AJ did whatever he wanted to do because of his dad's clout in the streets, but his dad's name meant nothing to me.

I wasn't the girl that fell apart at the sight of him. Don't get me wrong AJ was fine, light skin, thick curly hair, over six feet, cocky as fuck and money to blow. He was dreamy, to say the least, but his head was in the clouds, filled with whatever lies the yes crowd around him flooded his mind with. I'd never been the type to lie or sugar coat shit so, I stood out among the many females trying to be seen. I wasn't even pressed that he was fucking multiple females, his ex-included, the issue was he lied about it. I wasn't into sharing dick and I knew he had to get it somewhere, he wasn't my "man" so what did I care? It was the lies that I cut him for, if you lie about little shit then you'd lie about big shit too and that was a no go for me.

"We cool, it's no beef or nothing like that. I got a lot going on and I need to focus on me the next few weeks." I told her the lie I'd come up with.

Even though AJ and I hadn't had sex yet, he gained a lot of his popularity through social media. He loved taking pictures and keeping his followers updated on his moves and because of that, I'd gained a little hood following too. People loved seeing us out in public and were constantly speaking to him or just staring at us. He said it was because he didn't pay females attention like that outside of his long-time girlfriend, Christina. I just turned eighteen this past August, so I was in high school for a lot of the time while we were talking, but none of that mattered. It wasn't just the popularity that I missed though, I missed the drama with him. He was always so protective of me like he cared bout everything about me. Anytime a nigga looked at me too long or showed me any kind of attention he was talking shit, it made me feel special. I'd never had anybody treat me like I was a priority before and it wasn't a feeling I wanted to give up.

"Well, since we all single then, we need to go out this week-end," Money said sticking her tongue out.

"I really need to re-twist my hair——"

"You always say no, you can't go," Money pouted.

"Because I wasn't old enough before," I laughed.

"Okay, but you're old enough now and we all could use some time out, right?" she asked Khadija.

"Yeah, come on Sinna," Khadija encouraged with a wide smile.

"Okay, Friday night bitches," I agreed covering my face.

* * *

"Damn, you done fucking with me?" AJ asked leaning against the door frame.

He was standing in the same exact spot I met his ass in, his dimpled grin sent a tingle through me, but I quickly turned my head and focused back on putting Justyce's coat on. His mom, Ms. Dana ran a home daycare and since her rates weren't high like most people's and she seemed to really love kids, I brought Justyce to her. She tried to offer me an even bigger discount once she found out I was fucking with AJ, but I declined it. Even if I was the type of person to take hand-outs, I would never accept a discount because I was fucking her son.

"Hey AJ." I smiled at him even though I wanted to cuss his ass out.

"What's up with you? You playing games I see." He said as he stepped into the room.

"I'm playing games? How am I playing games?" I asked tilting my head to the side.

"You sitting here smiling at me now, but as soon as you leave you gone ignore my phone calls and text messages." He complained.

"I can't smile and speak when I see you?" I asked as I struggled to pick Justyce up.

His little legs kicked as he wiggled against me, trying to get out of my arms.

"You gon spoil that lil nigga. He can walk, stop babying the boy." He fussed over Justyce.

"Whatever." I replied holding Justyce's hand now that his feet were on the floor.

"So, what's up?" AJ asked as I walked past him.

"Ain't nothing up. I got a lot going on with my sister and you got your own shit to figure out." I shrugged.

"I ain't got shit to figure out." He spat.

"So, what's up with you and Christine?" I asked stopping to look him in the eyes.

"Me and *Christina* are cool." He shrugged.

"Cool enough to vacation together, right?" I asked with a smirk.

"It wasn't like that. I went to Miami and she ended up following me, that's it. It wasn't a vacation together." He explained.

And here was the problem, part of me wanted to believe him. I didn't want to admit to him that I logged in from Simone's page and saw all her pictures even the text messages they sent back and forth especially the one about catching "their" flight. Instead, I simply nodded my head agreeing with his excuse.

"Okay." I shrugged.

"That's it? So, we cool again?" he asked with a smile.

"Why wouldn't we be?" I frowned.

"Cool. Ima call you when I get to the crib." He smiled at me again.

I smiled back agreeing with him, secretly knowing I wouldn't answer another one of his phone calls again.

The rest of the week rushed by. The same old bullshit day in and day out until finally, it was Friday. Khadija agreed to re-twist and style my dreads, while Money picked out my outfit. I'd been boosting again, this time out of Rue 21, only I had a little help this time. I knew one of the sales associates who gave me an outfit for less than twenty dollars.

"I swear yo dreads so pretty even when they ain't twisted," Khadija said as I sat on the floor in her bedroom.

"Thank you, I really don't do much with them other than keep 'em clean," I shrugged.

"I wish I was brave enough to start dreads. I just can't go through that ugly stage girl. I'm already dark skin," she joked.

"Everybody has their own preference, some niggas like chocolate, others like caramel, shit most niggas love chocolate," I told her.

"Niggas love pussy, they'd fuck a tree if enough niggas said that shit was fire," Money said rolling her eyes.

"Speaking of niggas, where yo fine ass brother?" Money asked.

"Probably somewhere balls deep in a hoe," Khadija replied bucking her eyes.

"You need to stop trying to keep me and my baby fauva apart," Money told her rolling her eyes playfully.

"No, you need to stop being a hoe. Khalifa ain't thinking about you." Khadija called her out.

"I thought yo brother liked hoes though?" Money asked with a grin.

"Let my mama hear you talking like that and she gone put yo ass out. She was just running her mouth about him wrapping it up cause she wasn't raising his kids," Khadija replied.

"I ain't say I was trying to get pregnant tomorrow. We got time, I'm only nineteen," she rolled her eyes.

"You need some help." Khadija and I both laughed after she said it.

Finally, we were dressed and heading out the door when we walked through the living room only to be stopped by Khadija's older brother. I'd been over Khadija's house before, but I'd never met the infamous Khalifa. Khadija told me their mom sent Khalifa and their cousin to Atlanta to live with their father when she was thirteen, but he came home when their mom got sick.

"Where the fuck is the rest of that dress?" her brother asked, stopping us from moving forward.

My eyes bounced around the room and I was in shock to see Saint and Kidd from the other day sitting on the couch. Saint was wearing a black t-shirt with dark blue jeans and a pair of sneakers I'm sure cost more than I could afford. His eyes landed on mine and he formed a wide smile. I held my breath as I watched his eyes run over my body before he was forced to look away.

"Boy, you better watch yo damn mouth in my house!" Khadija's mom, Nikki scolded him as she came around the corner.

"Now where the fuck is the rest of that dress?" Ms. Nikki asked facing Khadija.

The dress was a little short, but in her defense, it only rode up when she walked. When she was standing still it was fine.

"Ma, it's a dress. I got a jacket, I got on high boots, so it's only a little bit of skin peeking out and I'm grown," she whined.

"You ain't that grown," Saint spoke up.

How did they all know each other? Was Khadija fucking him?"

"Y'all better tell her! She thinks just cause she got a little job and she about to start taking college classes she grown. The girl just learned how to wipe her ass, talking bout she damn grown," Ms. Nikki rolled her eyes as she turned around and headed out the living room.

"Where y'all going?" Khalifa barked.

"Why does it matter? You ain't going," she said crossing her arms across her chest.

"Then I guess y'all got dressed for nothing," he shrugged focusing his attention to the game on the huge flat-screen TV.

"Khalifa! I'm grown, you gotta stop treating me like a kid!" she stomped a foot as she spoke.

"Try me," he said pushing his body back in the recliner making it rock a little.

Money and I looked to Khadija to see what she was going to do. She motioned for us to follow her as the boys went back to playing the game. Once we were outside, we jumped in Money's beat-up Honda and headed to a club named, *Solais*. Once we made it to the club all our nervous energy began to fade away especially since Money used her fake ID to get a wristband for our drinks.

I usually only sipped when I was out in public, but I was feeling myself tonight, and before I knew it, I was putting my lips on my third drink. Seeing AJ off in the corner with some Great Value version of his ex pissed me off, so I tossed that one back too.

"You good? Maybe you should slow down," Khadija suggested.

"I'm good girl," I blew her off as I sat at the table we had.

Money was dancing beside the table while she studied the crowd and Khadija was sitting beside me dancing in her seat like she was auditioning to be a Mary J. Blige extra.

"Damn, I gotta pee," I groaned just as Money walked away to the bar.

"If you wait for Money to come back then I'll go with you," Khadija told me.

I knew she didn't want to leave our drinks and clutches on the table while we went to the bathroom. I glanced back at the packed bar and shook my head, it was no way I could hold my bulging bladder that long. I rose from my seat and headed to the bathroom. The line was longer than I thought it would be, so I ended up pushing a couple of girls out my way and heading into the stall ahead of them. After emptying my bladder, I planned to apologize to the hoes I pushed, but the second I stepped out the stall they were in my face talking shit.

"You think you better than us? You too good to wait in line or something?" the first girl asked propping her hand on her narrow hips.

"My fault, I really had to go that's all," I explained.

"Don't you think we all need to go really bad?" she asked rolling her eyes.

"Evidently not since y'all just standing around instead of getting out my way so you can get to the bathroom," I shrugged.

I pushed past the trio and headed to the sink to wash my hands. After washing my hands and using the last two paper towels in the dispenser, I headed out the door to hear the same bitches talking shit as I left out.

"Ima beat her ass." I said out loud as I headed back into the bathroom but was stopped by someone grabbing my arm.

"Last time I saw you, you were fighting. I need my girl to be a lover, not a fighter." Saint said entering my personal space with that sexy smirk that tickled my insides.

His presence took my breath away. He was taller than I remembered, sexier too.

"Yo girl ain't seem like much of a lover the last time I saw her." I told him stepping away from him.

"Nah, that situation done." he said shaking his head.

"It didn't seem too done a week or so ago," I reminded him.

"Two weeks or so ago I ain't know what I know now. What is it they say? Hindsight is twenty-twenty, right?" he asked with a smirk.

"That might not be yo girl, but I'm good on the drama," I said, pushing him back as he stepped forward.

"You should fuck with me baby," he told me, pulling me towards him.

Whatever cologne he was wearing was hypnotizing and even though my mind was screaming for me to walk away from him, my feet were planted in place.

"You look like you got a bunch of hoes, I'm good." I declined once more.

"Give a nigga yo number at least," he replied, gripping my ass in his massive hands.

"You want my number for what? To call me, fill my head up with lies, fuck me and drive me crazy like ole' girl? I'm not interested," I shrugged stepping out of his embrace again.

"Damn, you really ain't trying to fuck with a nigga, huh?" he asked, rubbing the goatee that was slowly growing in on his face.

"Enjoy your night, Saint," I told him before sashaying my ass back over to the table with my friends.

MINYON A.K.A MONEY

MINYON A.K.A MONEY

"I know yo ass ain't over twenty-one," his deep voice spoke in my ear.

I snapped my head back to see who was pressed against me with their lips pressed against my ear.

"Why you so close?" I spat as I turned around.

"My fault. You looking good Money." Khalifa tucked his bottom lip as he looked me over.

I hadn't told anybody about the night I spent in a *Holiday Inn* hotel room sweating two double beds out with Khalia a few months ago. He came across the *people you may know* section of my Facebook and he looked like he had some bread, so I sent him a friend request. Less than twenty-four hours he was in my messenger texting all types of freaky shit he wanted to do to me. My mind knew the time we spent together was strictly sex, it was my pussy that didn't understand why I couldn't ask to spend more time with him. I couldn't even be in the same room with him without soaking my panties.

"Thank you." I spoke over the music into his ear.

As I leaned into him my breasts brushed against his

muscular arm winding my body up even more.

"I ought to beat yo ass, you know that right?" he asked, no longer smiling as he looked at me.

The music around us was so loud I could barely make out what he was saying. The grimace on his face spoke louder than anything he could have ever said. He was upset with me or maybe he felt the sexual tension too. Maybe that's what had his jaw clenched tight between his teeth and the soft tissue on the inside of his cheek. The way he tightened his fist and relaxed it repeatedly while his eyes fixated on me made my body feel like it was on fire as I watched him watching me.

"I think I might like that," I flirted.

He stepped even closer to me, locking me in place by resting both hands on either side of the bar, preventing me from moving. He didn't have to worry about me trying to get away from him, I'd wanted to be this close or closer to him since the minute I saw him at the house earlier.

"Oh, you definitely gon like it," he damn near moaned in my ear.

He pulled back and flashed my fake ID in my face, blew me a kiss and walked away taking my ID with him.

"What can I get for you?" the bartender asked yelling for my attention.

I shook my head and backed away.

Khalifa's fine ass just cost me eighty-five dollars, but I couldn't wipe the smile from my face. Which was fucking with me cause money was my thing. I loved the way it smelled, the way it felt in my hand, even the way it spent, especially when it wasn't mine. I wasn't some lazy bitch out here waiting with her hand out, I knew how to get out and get it on my own too. That was the difference between me and the bitches that were coming around trying they best to be seen while Khalifa sat back basically ignoring them hoes. My mama taught me *if you ain't bringing something to the table, you an expense and don't know nigga want a woman bringing him more problems.*

I was the only child of Raye Sawyer and if anybody knew anything about her, then they knew she was a madam. She learned and perfected the art of seduction and everything she learned she taught me. When I was younger, she kept her business life and her life at home with me separate. By the time I was thirteen, she'd sat me down and explained "the game" to me. She was a single mom, but she took great care of me, I didn't want or need for anything. When I turned eighteen, she offered to bring me in under her wing, but I refused, and we've been bumping heads ever since.

"Oh my god! Can we go?" Khadija groaned when I sat back down at the table.

"Damn, y'all just really getting here ain't you?" Khalifa asked with a smirk.

He glanced at Khadija briefly before his eyes bounced back over to me. His long, thick locs danced around his rib cage as he leaned forward in the chair he was sitting in, smiling hard at me. The gold fronts in his mouth grabbed my attention and fed my fantasy of him posted between my thighs with my clit between his juicy lips and teeth shielded by gold fronts.

"You see something you like over here?" I asked, matching his smirk.

He bit down on his bottom lip and tossed his long dreads back with his eyes still focused on me.

"Are y'all serious right now?" Khadija asked, interrupting our stare off by leaning forward.

"Y'all ready?" Sinna asked looking from me to Khadija.

"Let's go," I confirmed, rising from my seat and following my girls out the club.

* * *

While I was dreaming about Khalifa's sex game someone was calling interrupting my dreams.

"Hello?" I asked groggily.

"Aye, you were sleep?" Sean asked.

I lifted my head off the pillow to look at the alarm clock beside my bed and saw it was four-fifty-two in the morning.

"It's five in the fucking morning, what you think I was doing?" I asked rolling my eyes.

"Damn, baby my bad. I saw yo Instagram pics from earlier and I just wanted to tell you how pretty you were looking," he lied.

I knew that nigga was lying. He was probably out partying all damn night and didn't want to go home and face the music with his baby mama. Usually, I didn't have a problem with helping Sean out with his dilemma, but the last time he spent the night was months ago. He texted me here and there, but not enough for me to be on the phone with him at five in the morning. And on top of all of it, the nigga was cheap, and he had too much going on for me to ever take him seriously.

"Well, thank you, but I'll call you when I wake up for the day," I yawned.

"Come on Money, you should let a nigga come put you to sleep," he told me.

And there was the reason for his phone call, he wanted some ass. Too bad I wasn't in the mood to give shit away, so unless he was offering something, he was on his own.

"If I let you come put me to sleep, what do I get out of the deal?" I asked.

"You gone get a nut just like I'ma get one, fuck you mean?" he asked full of confidence.

He had no reason to be so confident because he hadn't been able to make me cum before. The only way I came with him was when I used the vibrator I kept in the drawer beside my bed.

"Well, right now sleep overrules a nut, so I'm going back to sleep," I declined his offer.

"Aight, I'ma call you tomorrow," he replied sounding

defeated.

I hung up the phone and pushed it under my pillow as I closed my eyes and attempted to go back to sleep. After a minute or two of trying to go back to sleep, I gave up and reached into my nightstand for my vibrator. I grabbed my phone and went to my favorite porn website and watched Rico Strong dick down two pretty bitches in a threesome. I squeezed my eyes together tightly as my legs spread wider to give my vibrator a better angle. My head thrashed back and forth against the sheets as my legs began to cramp up. Seconds later, just before I was about to cum the batteries in my vibrator died.

"Grrr!" I growled as I pushed my head back into the pillow in frustration.

I tossed my vibrator to the empty space beside me and let the sound of the birds chirping outside my window lull me to sleep as the sun rose.

Later that day, Sinna called me and asked me to come to take her to work. When I first met Sinna I didn't know she so young. She was just in her senior year of high school, but no one would have known that if she didn't tell them. I had no respect for her sister because she sat back and watched Sinna damn near kill herself working twenty and sometimes thirty hours a week while she went to school. I felt bad for her when she dropped out of school, but I knew she would get her GED and get on her feet, if not for her, then for Justyce. She loved that little boy and would do anything for him. I blamed their auntie too cause she was right there and she didn't do shit to make Sinna's life any easier.

"What time you get off?" I asked her once she was sitting beside me in the car as I backed out the driveway.

"I'm closing. I took Veronica's hours," she said pulling her thick locks into a ponytail.

"Twelve hours shorty, go head." I dragged the sentence out like a rapper.

"I ain't got a choice. I got all tests and shit I gotta pay for, I gotta save money so we can move——"

"Sinna, I keep telling you, you can always come to take the other room at my house. I wouldn't even ask for half the rent," I told her.

"I can't leave my sister like that Money. I mean I appreciate it, I really do, but tax time right around the corner and I'ma make sure this year I save some of it," she shrugged.

"What you be doing to get tax money girl?" I asked her.

"I don't file, Simone carries me and Justyce. Well, I usually file her taxes for her cause she doesn't know what she doing," she replied rolling her eyes.

"Well, at least you got a plan. Shit, I need to figure out what I'm doing while I'm sitting here talking to you," I sighed as I pulled into the parking lot at our job.

"You good, you got family and friends that got your back, it's really just me out here," she told me.

"Nah, it might seem like that, but me and Khadija got you. I know we ain't known each other but a year, but none of us survive in this world without somebody," I told her.

"I appreciate that more than you know," she told me with a smile.

"No worries, what time you get off?" I asked.

"Khadija working with us tonight, she said we'd have a ride home, but she doesn't come in until four," she explained.

"Okay, call me tomorrow," I told her as she got out of the car.

* * *

After talking to Sinna, I felt the need to talk to my mama, so I pulled up to her house.

"Hey," Leah, one of my mama's hoes spoke to me when she opened the door.

"Hey, where my mama?" I asked as I stepped into the

house.

"In her room," she said eyeing me.

I walked through the house filled with bitches walking around in their tank tops and panties until I made it to my mama's room. I knocked on her door and waited for her to tell me to come in.

"Who is it?" she asked almost thirty seconds later.

"Money," I replied.

The door popped open and I had to step back so some Chinese looking girl could walk past me.

"Ma, you still fucking these little girls?" I asked before I closed the door.

I knew that would get under her skin, but she was too old to be out here lying to these young girls and then pimping they dumb asses out.

"Money close my damn door!" she yelled from behind the bathroom door.

I laughed but did what she asked and sat down on the couch across from the bed with the tousled blankets on it.

"What you come all the way to Greensboro for?" she asked stepping out of the bathroom drying her wet hands with a towel.

"Damn, I can't come see my mama?" I asked eyeing her.

She was wearing some black jeans that hung loosely off her ass, a black V-neck t-shirt and a red leather vest like she was about to be in 90's music video. Her short baby afro was gelled to perfection making her look like the stud she was.

"It ain't like you fuck with me that often." she shrugged.

"Well, Christmas is right around the corner," I smirked.

"Let me Cash App you some money now," she huffed as she moved over to the bar in the corner of her room.

"So, sweet," I laughed joining her at the bar.

I watched her intently as she poured our drinks. She handed me a glass, tossed hers back and then focused on me as I did the same.

"What?" I asked her.

"What you doing with the rest of your life?" she asked me.

"I don't know I haven't quite figured it out yet. Why?" I asked watching her toss back another shot of Hennessy.

"You sitting around wasting your good years working in some bum ass fast food restaurant." she frowned.

"My good years? Ma—"

"Nah, don't Ma me. You wanted to make your own money, I let you. You wanted your own space, I let you move into your own space. I give it to you, I didn't expect you to last this long on your own, but Money it's been a year. What are you doing?" she asked as if shew as disappointed.

She was disappointed I wasn't following in her footsteps and stringing a bunch of women along, selling them dreams by the boatload in exchange for them selling pussy in my name. Yeah, technically it was an escort business, but the truth remained it was pussy being sold as well.

"I'm figuring it out, I'm making a life for myself." I explained.

"What kind of life is working eight hours a day on your feet, dealing with rude ass customers, and selling fast food all day? Ain't you tired of that shit?" she asked.

"Ten years from now—"

"Ten years from now you'll be married with a bunch of little kids hanging off a pair of old, saggy ass titties." She picked at me.

"You know what? I'll take it. It'll be better than living some pimp daddy lifestyle like you." I blurted out.

"This pimp daddy lifestyle raised yo ass! You can't avoid the inevitable, Money." She told me standing toe to toe with me.

"It's never going to happen." I scoffed.

"You better fall in line, pussy runs the world baby, believe that," she told me.

3

———

KHADIJA

"Do you ever go home?" I groaned as I walked into the kitchen.

Saint was sitting at the kitchen table eating a bowl of cereal and texting away on his phone.

"This is home, girl. You good? Heard you in the bathroom throwing up." He said looking up at me.

"I'm straight." I lied.

I wasn't straight, I was pregnant, and I knew it, but I didn't want to say anything because I knew I'd have to hear everybody's mouth about my decision. Yeah, I was grown, but the people in this house still treated me like a little ass girl. And I knew it would kill my mama. After busting her ass my entire life working two jobs to take care of me and Khalifa, she started having issues with her back. It was so bad now, she had trouble standing on her feet for more than an hour or so. It broke my dad's heart to see her so fragile, but he was also pissed cause he was sending money and she was gambling it away instead of spending it on us.

"I know when you lying nigga." He told me.

"I'm pregnant." I blurted out.

It was no point in trying to hide it from Saint, he was my cousin, but he was also my oldest friend. He knew all my secrets and he kept them without any issues and that's how our bond stayed all these years. But based on the look he was giving me now, I wish I hadn't said a word.

"Khadija! You let that nigga—"

"Saint, please. I feel bad enough already." I hung my head as I cut him off.

"You feel bad enough already? You ain't felt shit, yet Nikki gone kill you and that's only after Khalifa kills you first. And then Uncle David? Yeah, I don't want to be nowhere around for none of those conversations." He replied.

"I know. I fucked up." I said lowly.

"You gon keep it?" he whispered.

"I don't know yet." I told him just as my mama walked into the kitchen.

* * *

"Dirty, I told you I had to work at four today!" I hissed into the phone as I sat outside on the porch.

I was dressed in my Wendy's uniform waiting for my baby daddy to come to take me to work. I could have asked Khalifa or Saint to take me, but after their little pop-up visit at the club, I wasn't talking to Khalifa. I was grateful Khalifa and Saint were back in North Carolina after living in Atlanta with our dad, but they were doing too much.

Khalifa, Saint, and Kidd decided they were going to jump in the street game and sell dope when they were fourteen, they got possession charges and my dad made Saint and Khalifa go live with him and my mama was all for it. I missed my brother and my cousin while they were gone, and I wanted them home. Now, that them niggas were here minding my business I was ready for them to go back.

I closed my eyes and took a deep breath hoping to let go of all the angry energy I had built up inside of me. The sound of a car stopping in front of me prompted my eyes to pop open hoping it was my baby daddy. My face dropped seeing Kidd's long frame climb out of the all-white Challenger he drove.

"What up?" he asked as he walked over to me.

While Saint and Khalifa went to daddy boot camp, Kidd and I got to know each other. He hung around the house helping my mama with shit, taking out the trash, cutting the grass little shit like that. When he came over, I made sure he ate good, and he'd spent more than a few nights teaching me about college basketball. He could have been on the court playing for Duke, but after the drug possession charge and then the domestic violence charge, he picked up less than a year later, he didn't even try to get his scholarship back.

"Hey, what you about to do?" I asked him rising to my feet.

"Not shit," he shrugged.

"Can you take me to work?"

"Yeah, come on," he told me, motioning for me to follow him to his car.

Once we were in his car, he plugged his phone in and he pressed a few buttons on his phone and some old school Kanye filled the speakers.

"Nigga, what you know about this?" I laughed, turning the volume up a little bit.

"More than yo young ass," he smirked at me.

"Yeah, yeah, yeah," I blew him off with a laugh.

We danced and performed a few songs before finally pulling up to my job.

"Thank you so much for the ride Kidd, I really appreciate it," I told him as I turned to face him in the leather seat.

"You good, you know you ain't gotta thank me for this shit, I got you. What time you get off?" he asked.

"I'ma try to get Khalifa or Saint to pick me up later if my boyfriend doesn't come," I replied.

"You really just gone say that shit in front of me?"

"You really just flaunt the bitches you fucking in front of me." I shrugged.

"You see me claiming any of them though? You already know I'm waiting on you." He told me.

"Yeah, that's what yo mouth say." I said blowing him off.

"Why you keep fucking with that lame ass nigga?" Kidd asked.

"Kidd, I don't comment on the dusty ass hoes you been seen fucking with," I reminded him.

"Nah, you can't do that cause I ain't here playing myself like that," he laughed.

"Damn, I'm playing myself by fucking with him?" I asked feeling a little hurt.

I didn't know what information he had, but I knew my nigga wasn't perfect. He had a baby mama I couldn't stand, but other than a few questionable offenses and run-ins with her I didn't have any proof of anything else.

"Look, all I'm saying is you deserve better and you know it," he shrugged.

Did I deserve better? What would classify as better? Dirty was out here grinding just like Kidd was, but Dirty worked directly with AJ. Ace treated his son like the next coming of Jesus and sadly so did the streets, so Dirty had money and connections. He was fine as all hell, with a seductive smile mixed with a thuggish demeanor and a big ole' horse dick swinging between his legs. A few strokes of that motherfucka could have the strongest bitch ready to fight till the death for the dick.

"I love him Kidd, he's not what everyone thinks he is," I insisted.

"For yo sake, I hope so," he nodded his head and faced forward in the car.

I climbed out and headed into my job to start my shift.

* * *

"Sorry I'm late," I cringed as I walked in avoiding the eyes of my manager as I clocked in.

"That's what, twice in the past week?" my manager asked.

"I know Ms. Janice and I'm sorry, but it won't happen again," I told her as I moved to the back to set my purse down.

"Finally," Sinna said bumping me playfully as I passed her.

I stuck my tongue out at her playfully as I continued making my way to the back of the store.

"Can I talk to you for a moment, please?" Ms. Janice asked joining me in the break room.

I rolled my eyes but turned to face her bracing myself for any slick shit, she was about to spew out her mouth.

"Khadija, I'm not trying to be hard on you or treat you any different or none of that, but you really gotta stop this late thing. Today it was twenty minutes, but a few days ago it was ten minutes—" she started to explain, but I cut her off.

"I already said I was sorry and that I would work on it. I don't have a car right now, but I'll do my best from this point on, okay?" I asked, staring her dead in the eye.

I hated when I had to bite my tongue, but I knew I needed to keep this job if I didn't want to hear my mama's mouth about how she worked two or three jobs when she was my age. I love my mama, God knows I do, but she could work a nerve like no other. She let Khalifa do damn near whatever he wanted, but me, nah, I had to do what she said, and he got to do what he wanted. I didn't feel like any of the stupid shit was fair, but my mama's rule was, *"boys created babies and girls brought 'em home."*

"I can't point out everybody else's issues and then overlook yours. I know you're trying, and I appreciate your effort, but if you're having trouble getting to work then we can cut back on your hours if you want," she told me.

"I'll be on time from here on out," I told her brushing past her and leaving her in the breakroom.

After Christmas, I was going to find another job cause I was over this shit.

"Girl, you seen my club pics?" one of my coworkers, Melanie asked one of the girls beside me.

I didn't waste my time getting to know any of the employees that worked here cause they either didn't last long or lasted too long and thought they walked on water or some shit.

"Yes, bitch you looking, good girl. You keep going to the gym like you are and you ain't gone have to get that lipo," the second girl slapped hands with the first.

"Excuse me, sir!" a customer yelled out as a guy wearing a ski mask over his face stepped in front of her in line.

The quick weave in the woman's head was three different colors of oranges and I guess it was supposed to be a fade-in of some sort, but it didn't compliment her dark brown complexion in the least. Her smooth brown cheeks quickly turned rosy red as her eyes filled with fear.

"EVERYBODY PUT YO MOTHERFUCKING HANDS UP!" the guy yelled materializing a gun from out of nowhere.

I raised my hands doing exactly what the guy asked of me. Seconds later, another shooter came in and headed over to the register. My heartbeat out my chest and my legs knocked together as I struggled to keep myself from fainting.

"EMPTY BOTH THEM MOTHERFUCKAS!" the masked robber boomed referring to the register in front of me.

Sinna was already emptying her cash register, so I moved

to the counter on wobbly legs and started putting the cash in the bags the masked robber handed me.

"Hurry the fuck up!" he barked banging his gun on the stainless-steel counter.

"Okay, okay." Sinna raised her hands and handed him the bag full of money.

The crowd erupted in screams as they did what he asked of them. I moved slowly doing as I was told before I was stopped.

"Now, everybody get on the fucking ground!" the first guy replied firing two quick shots into the air.

The crowd erupted in screams as they did what he asked of them.

"Nah, not you two behind the register. Both y'all get out here," the second one replied pointing at me and Sinna.

The first guy snatched Sinna by her elbow and pushed her towards the double glass doors. I backed away from the second guy who was approaching me.

"No, please!" I begged as he motioned for me to come with him.

"Get moving!" he boomed.

My feet betrayed me as they moved forward until Sinna and I were standing side by side in front of the double doors.

"Nice doing business with y'all," the second man laughed and even though his face was covered by a ski mask I could tell he was smiling.

"BRING YO ASSES THE FUCK ON." The second man yelled at us, both Sinna and I stood there too terrified to move.

The first guy pushed the gun into my back and my feet began to move towards the door.

Lord, please let me make it home.

SINNA

SINNA

Scared, frightened, petrified, alarmed, horrified.

I was all of those things. I didn't know what to do or what to say as two strangers pushed me and Khadija in the backseat of a two-door green Explorer. I wanted to run away screaming, run back inside the building and lock the doors, something, but the fear of being shot kept my ass moving into the backseat silently.

"Please don't hurt me, please," Khadija pleaded with them as she was being pushed into the truck beside me.

The first guy pushed the gun he was holding into Khadija's face silencing her instantly. Seconds later the truck was moving, and we were driving down capital like nothing happened.

"Where y'all taking us?" Khadija asked.

"To hell, if you don't shut the fuck up, sit back and mind yo business," the nigga in the passenger seat spoke without turning around to look at Khadija.

"Shh, they still have their masks on, they don't want us to know who they are," I told her bumping her thigh.

Not even a full second later both niggas pulled the masks from their faces as they continued driving.

"Oh shit!" Khadija whispered.

"What? You know them?" I panicked.

"No, but they gone kill us if they letting us see their faces!" she blurted out no longer whispering.

"Ain't nobody gone kill yo loud ass." The second guy spoke.

I wasn't listening to shit he was saying cause Khadija was making sense. I dug my nails into the driver's eyes making him swerve and almost hit another car. Suddenly, chaos filled the car, Khadija was screaming, I was screaming and the nigga in the passenger seat was trying to steer the car. Somehow, we managed to pull over and turn into a Walmart parking lot.

"GET THE FUCK OUT THE CAR!" The dude in the passenger side seat yelled pointing a gun at both Khadija and me.

We both slowly got out of the car with both hands raised high. I studied the nigga standing beside the car, that was once driving he was short and bald-headed, but after I inspected him a little more I noticed he didn't have any hair on his face, not even his eyebrows.

"Arms out," the passenger spoke to me.

He had a short baby afro with curly hair, his light skin was riddled with blemishes and bumps, but he moved as if he didn't know he was ugly as hell.

"What?" I frowned.

My eyes dropped down to his hands that held zip ties and the ski masks they were using earlier.

"I promise you, we not gone say nothing. Just leave us here, I promise you we ain't gone tell nobody shit," I explained as tears filled my eyes.

"We can do this the easy way, or we can do this the hard way, it's up to you," he told me.

I swallowed the lump in my throat and extended my arms

out, so he could put the zip ties on and covered my face with the ski mask. Just before the ski mask went over my face the backward way, I locked eyes with Khadija. The expression on her face matched what was going on inside of me.

"Preciate y'all boys." A voice called out just as the ski mask went over my face.

I know that voice!

"AJ?" I asked out loud and snatched the ski mask off my face.

"Come here baby." AJ called out to me.

I watched Khadija take hers off and race to the passenger side of the car AJ was hanging out of.

"How are you here right now?" I asked with a frown.

"You wouldn't talk to me, I had to get your attention somehow." He shrugged.

"You dumb ass!" I screamed hitting him repeatedly.

"CALM YO ASS DOWN!" he barked pulling my body close to him.

"Let me go!" I screamed attempting to get away from him.

"You causing a scene right now." He growled focusing on me.

"Why would you do this? They could have killed somebody!" I snapped pushing him again.

"But they didn't. I just wanted your attention, that's all." He shrugged.

"So, robbery and kidnapping just seemed like the only way to get my attention?" I asked looking at him.

"Look, I thought you was gon laugh when you found out. I didn't think you were going to be upset." He shrugged.

"Leave me alone, AJ." I huffed as I moved away from him.

"Hold up, where you going?" he asked attempting to pull me back to him.

"Away from you. You could have picked me up from work, sent me flowers, hell left candy for me at home, shit anything, but this! This is crazy as hell, don't you get that?" I frowned.

"I mean—"

"See, you don't get it! Until you do, stay away from me!" I yelled pushing his muscular chest away from me.

* * *

"Y'all good?" Khalifa asked when he picked us up.

"Yeah," Khadija asked as we climbed into the truck with him and Saint.

"Sinna, you good?" Saint's voice was in my ear, but my mind was miles away.

Saint's big hands grabbed my chin and forced me to turn and look at him. His eyes were wide, filled with worry and concern. His dreads were styled into a new style like a crown giving him a regal type vibe. It felt like every time I saw Saint, he looked better each time.

"I'm good," I confirmed for him.

"You don't look like it. You wanna talk?" he asked.

I shrugged my shoulders. I did want to talk, but I didn't know what I wanted to say yet. I kept going over the look in AJ's eyes that he was amused that I was scared. He actually thought the shit was funny, everybody from Wendy's was probably scared to death and AJ thought the shit was funny.

"Look at me," Saint demanded.

My eyes slowly landed on him, maintaining his intense stare.

"It's over. You know that shit, right? It's over with it," he attempted to console me.

But it wasn't over for me.

"Can you teach me how to shoot a gun?" I asked, speaking over the music.

"I got you. Let me know when you ready," he told me agreeing.

Several hours later, I was exhausted from lying to the

police about who abducted us and how we got away. I planned to strangle AJ the next time I saw him.

"Damn, I'm tired as fuck," I complained as I walked up the front steps to my Auntie's house.

"You had a crazy day," Saint offered as he followed behind me.

"True," I nodded.

"Take a couple of days off and relax," he ordered.

"I plan to, but I'll call you about the gun range," I told him.

"You ain't even got my phone number." He grinned stepping closer to me. "Put your number in my phone," he said passing me the Galaxy phone.

"Why are you walking around with a damn Android?" I frowned.

"I ain't never had an iPhone," he shrugged.

"Nigga, let me upgrade you," I joked as I typed my number in his phone.

I knew something crazy was coming out of his mouth when he grinned at me, but he never got a chance to say anything before the front door came flying open and out came a barely dressed Simone.

"Sinna! Are you okay? I heard what happened on the news!" she cried.

Her attention started on me, but by the time she was done talking she was solely focused on Saint. And this pussy-hungry motherfucka had the nerve to blush while she eyed him.

"I'm fine Simone," I replied lowly.

"Well, I see that," she grinned.

The crop top she wore exposed her pudgy stomach and the small boy shorts she had on exposed the bottom half of her ass cheeks. Saint's eyes navigated back to mine and he pulled me towards him for a hug.

"Don't be ignoring my phone calls or we gone have a problem," he told me before he let me go and walked off.

"Bye," Simone sang as I walked into the house.

"Where Auntie?" I asked looking around the apartment.

"She said she was working late, but I think she might have had a date or something," she shrugged.

"Where Justyce?" I wondered since I didn't hear him playing.

"Dirty came by and got him," she said like it was a normal occurrence.

"WHAT?" I asked stopping in my tracks.

Yeah, Dirty was his dad, but he hadn't spent anyone on one, alone time with him before now. What the fuck was wrong with Simone?

"Why would you let him go with him?" I frowned.

"Because that's his daddy! That's fucking why!" she screamed at me.

"And the nigga next door has seen Justyce more than him. Why would you let him take him?" I asked shaking my head.

"Just because you buy him shit don't make you his mama," she told me.

"Oh, now that's all I do? He's three and if it wasn't for me, he wouldn't even be potty trained! He wouldn't know his colors or—"

"All that shit he learned in daycare! You think you doing something special because you walk around here babying him all the fucking time?" she asked rolling her eyes.

"I pay for his daycare, I wake him up, make sure he gets there and gets picked up. Half the time you walk around like he doesn't exist!" I hissed.

"I don't give a fuck what you think, that little boy came out my pussy! Until you push one out you can't tell me shit about raising him!" she yelled at me.

"You know what? I keep trying to be there for you and help you cause you're my sister and I love you, but you fight me at each turn. When we were younger you helped me, you cared about how I felt, but now? Now, you just don't give a fuck about nothing but Simone," I told her.

"Girl go head with yo dramatic ass," she blew me off.

"And yo Auntie said if she catches Dirty's ugly ass in her house again she gone put us all out," I told her.

"I'm a grown-ass woman and I gotta creep around like a fucking kid just so my son can spend time with his daddy. Just so I can get some dick, how the fuck is that fair?" she asked.

"And what about the baby you're carrying? Is she supposed to just look the other way now that you got another baby coming?" I asked her.

"By the time I have my baby we'll be in our own place," she shrugged.

"You think that makes the shit okay? It's okay to make kids when you can't take care of the one you already got?" I asked her.

"Who is it with the problem you or her?" she asked propping her hand on her wide hips.

"Simone, we live in her house! We moved into her house because we couldn't keep up with the bills, we had in our own house," I reminded her.

"We buy food, we pay the cable bill and clean up and—"

"And it's still her house!" I yelled.

"You would agree with her," she scoffed.

"Because she's right! It's her house, she makes the rules and we just gotta follow 'em," I shook my head.

"Well, we can just stay until tax time and then we can move," she shrugged walking past me.

I was all argued out. I didn't know what else to say to her to get her to understand where our Auntie was coming from. After a long shower, I climbed in the queen size bed that almost took up most of the space in the small room and took my ass to sleep.

Later that night, I was jolted awake by the sound of the front door slamming shut. I sat up in the bed and wiped my eyes before I looked beside me to see a sleeping Justyce next to me. I checked the time on my phone and saw I had two text messages waiting.

SIMONE: I'll be back in the morning.

AJ: Let's start over, let me take you out tomorrow.

* * *

"TT, want ceeroll," Justyce said pushing me.

I opened my eyes and smiled seeing his little hands lightly tugging on my dreads. I pulled his hands out of my dreads and kissed his palm. I sat up, grabbed my bonnet and headed to the bathroom to pee before I went to get him situated with breakfast.

"Simone, where are you?" I asked into my phone, cradling it on my shoulder as I moved around the kitchen.

"I'll be home around check out time," she replied and hung up the phone.

"This bitch," I whispered.

"How you feeling this morning?" my Auntie asked as she walked into the kitchen.

"I'm okay," I lied.

After the fight with Simone, I was ready to just wash my hands with her. Literally, the only thing saving her was my nephew.

"Where's Simone?" she asked as she made her coffee.

"I don't know," I shrugged.

"You haven't talked to her?" she asked.

"I know she's out, but I don't know her location or nothing," I explained.

She nodded her head as she sipped the hot liquid from the coffee cup in her hand that read, *No talking before coffee*. I closed my eyes and wished she read her own cup before she poured coffee in it.

"I heard on the radio it's a job fair down at the community college today," she said lowly.

"I'll make sure to let her know," I told her.

She played with Justyce for a few minutes before the awkwardness in the room drove her out of the kitchen. I was grateful for my Auntie, I really was, but being here in her house just reminded me that I needed to have a plan for my life, having a job at Wendy's was cool, but I needed more than just Wendy's.

* * *

After I got myself and Justyce dressed for the day, I got ready to take him with me to the job fair. As soon as we stepped outside to walk up the block to the bus stop my phone started ringing with a *blocked* number on the display, but I knew it was AJ.

"Yes?"

"What's up beautiful." AJ's deep baritone tickled my eardrum.

"Why are you on my phone?" I frowned as I asked.

"I just wanted to tell you I'm sorry again. I miss you yo." He told me.

"You really think you so smooth, huh?" I asked as I pulled my face away from the screen to see the cash app notification. "Five hundred dollars?" I asked in disbelief.

"You really think you so smooth, huh?"

"I ain't trying to be smooth," he denied it, but I could hear the smile in his voice.

"What you doing today?" I asked him.

"I'm trying to fuck with you," he flirted.

"I'm spending the day with my nephew it seems," I exhaled as I watched Justyce play on the bench at the bus stop.

"Where yo sister at?" he asked.

I didn't have an answer for him because it was almost one

in the afternoon and well past check out time. Knowing Simone, it was no telling what her ass was up to. I called her phone a few times and she ignored my calls and didn't respond to my text message like I was a bill collector or something. I didn't have time to keep playing with her, so I brought Justyce with me to the job fair.

"I don't know, but I'll call you later," I replied.

"Aight," he told me just as the bus pulled up.

* * *

By the time I made it back home, it was almost six and Justyce was knocked out after I had him walking around beside me instead of holding him.

"Hey," Simone spoke as I walked past her on the couch.

"Hey," I replied dryly.

"How long he been sleep? You know he can't be sleep this late or he gone be up forever," she told me as if she would be the one up in the middle of the night with him.

"He just really dozed off on the walk home," I told her.

"The walk? Where y'all been?" she frowned.

"I went to the job fair at the community college and then we went walking around and just enjoyed the city. We went to the park, we just had fun," I shrugged.

"Well, I'm glad he was able to get out of the house, he be cooped up in the house with crazy pants all the time," she explained.

"Simone, are we going to talk about this baby situation again?" I asked her.

"What is there left to say?" she hissed rising from her seat making herself a plate of food.

"It's a lot of shit left to say. We can't afford a baby right now, we can barely afford us and you really not on birth control?" I asked her in disbelief.

I got on birth control the second I decided I wanted to

have sex. I was probably the only virgin in high school popping birth control pills on time.

"When do we have money for me to pick up birth control?" she asked rolling her eyes.

"Condoms don't cost but what, a dollar?" I pointed out.

"Maybe for them lil pencil dick niggas you be fucking." She scoffed.

"Well, if the nigga can't afford to wrap it up then her probably can't afford to take care of a baby." I pointed out.

"I'm really getting fed up with the twenty questions. I have a child already, clearly, I don't use condoms. What you want me to do about it now?" she shrugged as if nothing I was saying even registered with her.

"Is he the only nigga you fucking raw at least?" I asked.

I couldn't help but be worried about her. She was moving recklessly as if nothing she was doing mattered, but it did. It really did. What if Dirty was out fucking other chicks raw and gave her something? He was the type of man to go from one chick to another with no regard to anything other than the nut he was getting right then, but Simone didn't see that.

"Sinna!" she snapped, raising both hands in the air.

"You fucking this nigga and you basically homeless. Where does he live? Why doesn't he take care of you? He loves you so much," I asked her.

I wasn't trying to rub the shit in her face, I really wasn't. I was trying to get her to understand that she was fucking a man that didn't care about her well-being. When she pulled her missing stunts, it was always with him, but without their son. She couldn't explain it or defend it, so she chose to attack me.

"First of all, Dirty has offered Justyce and me a place beside him in his bed every night on several occasions, I declined the offer to help you," she said like I was the one holding us down.

"He offered you a bed in his mama's house? The nigga

still lives with his mama, Simone, what can he do for you?" I asked her.

"That's why you should mind yo business, he got an apartment now!" she spat.

"Well, by all means, do what you gotta do and go live with him." I dared her.

She nodded her head and laughed before she spoke again, "We'll be gone by morning."

"Good luck," I replied refusing to allow my pride to get in the way.

4

MONEY

"Your body is fucking amazing," my date complimented me.

"Thank you," I grinned at him as his eyes assaulted my body.

I grabbed his extended hand and allowed him to lead me to his luxury car. The sleek all-black Porsche was sexy as hell. Just the sight of my dream car made my nipples hard. I didn't know what a square like Demarcus was doing driving such a dope ass car, but he was, and it was little mysterious shit like this that kept me going out with him. After a long conversation with my mom, I was more pressed than ever to find a guy to settle down with. I was cool with dating for meals, bags, and followers on social media. I was a hustler just like my mom, but I couldn't do the shit she was doing. It was a difference between flat out selling pussy and dating for stability.

Demarcus was a nerdy, IT guy that was looking for some arm candy and he was willing to pay a shit ton of money on my hair, clothes, makeup and whatever else I requested before

I was "presentable" for him. He was going to pay somebody to do it, why shouldn't it be me?

"So, where to?" I asked flashing a smile.

"Somewhere special, let me take care of you." He winked and pressed the push to start.

At first, the idea bothered me. Then my mother reminded me that pussy been on sale since the beginning of time. It wasn't like I had a nigga at the time anyway, so why not let enjoy spending time with a nigga? Hell, I was pretty, smart, and I had a body that could make the most innocent nigga think guilty thoughts. Growing up, I watched my mama treat women like shit, she fucked 'em and sent 'em on their way. Watching her act like that helped me keep a guard around my heart. Most niggas felt like knocking that wall down was too much work.

I didn't think I was going to like dealing with squares, but after dating a few of them I'd learned how to vet them, but I still kept a blade and a taser in my purse in case a nigga tried to jump stupid. I was determined to find a stable relationship, I needed to prove to my mama, but she was wrong.

Demarcus took me to Ruth Chris in an attempt to impress me I'm sure. I'd done a background check already and the other thing that impressed me about him was that he was married. I couldn't believe that a man that looked like he did, dressed like he did, and spoke as well as he did could be dogging his wife out like he was. His wife was actually the breadwinner between the two of them. She bought him the pussy magnet of a car he was driving, she probably bought the designer suit his athletic body was poured into. Apart of me felt bad for her, but not bad enough to turn down a meal.

"So, Minyon, you never told me what you were in school for," Demarcus started the conversation once we were seated and he'd ordered a bottle of the restaurant's Moscato.

I knew he wanted sex, not just because of his choice of restaurant or price of wine, but because he remembered the things we talked about. I told him I didn't drink much wine, but when I did, that it had to be light, anything Moscato basically. I told him that I'd never been to the restaurant everyone always talked about. I was doing my best not to give him credit for the things he was doing because I knew he had a wife.

"Finance," I lied.

I had no idea what type of line I would be getting with that response, all I knew were men thought boss women were sexy, so I tossed it out there.

"That's smart," he smiled, seemingly impressed by my answer.

"What do you do for a living?" I asked him.

"I'm in construction," he told me.

Our conversation was interrupted by the waiter offering us our food. I dove into the tender steak and loaded baked potato without saying anything. After a few more stabs of food, I glanced up to see Demarcus staring at me with an amused expression.

"What?" I asked with a smile.

"You're so pretty," he complimented me.

I put my fork down and looked him in the eyes.

"I tried not to say anything because I didn't want to be all in your business, but I know you're married," I blurted out.

"Is that an issue for you?" he asked.

"Is it an issue for your wife? I don't want to cause any issues between those two of you," I explained.

This was supposed to be about filling my time with something other than the next ain't shit nigga that wanted to fuck me and would never love me.

"My wife and I have somewhat of an open relationship. She can enjoy what she likes while I enjoy what I like," he told me.

"So, you just fuck other people and stay together?" I asked.

"Basically, it's just sex," he shrugged.

"Damn," I replied.

His answer left me speechless. I expected him to lie about his situation, tell me he was separated, tell me he had no plans on staying with his wife, but he'd shown me something different when he told me the truth.

"You seem surprised," he replied clearly amused by my expression.

"I am. I didn't expect you to tell me that. I expected a denial," I confirmed.

"I can be many things, but the one thing I won't do is lie. I'm a very busy man, I'm working on building an empire, so I have a lot on my plate, I don't have the time to remember a lie. I realize my situation may make you uncomfortable and I understand if you don't want to see me again," he said.

"I'm adjusting to this idea. What is it that you want from me?" I asked him.

"I'm not asking for anything, but your time. Anything else you want to give me is entirely up to you," he replied.

"Let's be clear about what you're asking me. You want me to basically be your side chick?"

"If you have to put a tittle on it, you can call it whatever you want," he shrugged.

"You want me to be your girlfriend and your wife will just be okay with that?" I wondered out loud.

"It would be hard for her to be in her feelings about it since she has a girlfriend and a boyfriend," he explained.

"And that's okay with you? For your wife to have sex with people that aren't you?" I asked.

"It's how we've lived our lives for years," he explained.

I nodded my head but kept my mouth closed while I let his words run around my mind.

"We don't have to continue talking about it, let's just get to know each other and if we get to that point then we'll get to that point," he shrugged.

* * *

The next day Sinna, Khadija and I sat across my bed while I told them about my date with Demarcus. Apart from me felt like I shouldn't get involved with him because he was married. I wanted to get married, buy a house, have kids, the dog, and the white picket fence, I wanted it all.

"I say do it," Khadija said with a shrug. "Niggas cheat all the time, I don't understand what the big issue is," she said picking up the soft pink fingernail polish and painting one of her nails.

"Don't do it. Put yourself in her shoes?" Sinna asked.

"All niggas cheat," Khadija said with a shrug.

"Aw shit, what Derrick do now?" I asked.

"I told him I missed my period, you know just to feel him out? This nigga told me to get an abortion." she said rolling her eyes.

"Hold up, bitch you're pregnant?" I asked narrowing my eyes at her.

"Yeah, but I don't know what to do honestly." she hung her head.

"What do you want to do? You don't have to do shit he's asking you to do. Fuck him." Sinna frowned.

"It's like I know I should walk away from him, but he has such a stronghold on me." she shrugged.

"What did your brother say?" I asked her.

"I haven't told any of my family yet, well I told Saint, but that's it." She shrugged.

"Having a baby shouldn't be something your sad about, you should be happy and celebrating, you're bringing a life into the world." Sinna said throwing a small smile Khadija's way.

"And then it's the issue about money. He asked me to borrow fifty dollars the other week, so I gave it to him. You know trying to be understanding and loyal and shit, I don't mind looking out, you know?" she explained.

"Please, don't tell me you basically ended up paying this nigga to get you pregnant cause he ain't got the money to pay you back, right?" I asked trying not to laugh at her facial expression telling me everything I said was right.

"What a waste," Sinna spat laughing out loud.

"Shit, that nigga got a self-employed business. He the CEO at Dick 'em down. You pay 'em, he slay 'em." I laughed.

"I hate you," Khadija said throwing a pillow my way.

"Simone moved out," Sinna said out loud.

"No, she didn't," I said leaning forward to listen to Sinna.

"Yes, she did. She packed all her shit and all Justyce's shit and moved in with her baby daddy. I don't know what her and him doing." Sinna said rolling her eyes.

"She just up and left without saying anything?" I asked.

"No, we got into it, she's pregnant. What did she expect me to say to her? We struggling to make it on a daily basis, I'm out here stealing clothes and shit and she laying up in my Auntie's house letting that nigga fuck her and get her pregnant," she groaned holding her face.

"Well, shit I saw let her be grown and handle her business. It ain't like she was really helping you anyway. You can't save grown people." I shrugged.

"And what about Justyce?" Khadija asked raising her eyebrows.

"What about him? That's her son, I know you love him, Sinna, but you gotta let her handle her business." I shrugged.

"I can't help, but feel like Money's right, she kept saying she was Justyce's mama not me. I'm gone miss Justyce, but I'll still stop by and pick him up every few days, but I'm done trying to take care of my sister. I love her to the moon and back, but I gotta start worrying about myself. I'm the one sitting here trying to get a GED, she couldn't care less that she ain't got a GED or high school diploma." Sinna replied shaking her head and making her dreads bounce.

"Damn, I'm sorry, I didn't know y'all had some real-life shit going on," I told them as I rolled a blunt.

"After Christmas, I'm going to the community college to register for some classes. I need to find something else to focus on. After I pass this last test of course." Sinna said with a smile.

"I'm proud of you," I told her.

"We should all register for school, what else we got going on?" Sinna asked.

"I'm scared, but I'ma do it." I agreed.

SINNA

SINNA

"You finally made some time for a nigga," AJ said as I sat down at the table across from him.

"You forget I was mad at you." I reminded him.

He wasn't dressed to impress, but he was presentable. Just a plain black button-up and a pair of khaki's, nothing too special. He wasn't wearing the flashy jewelry that got him lots of attention, he looked more down to Earth today.

"You look good baby," he complimented me.

"Thank you." I replied squirming in the stolen mini dress I was wearing that rode up my hips.

"How you been?" He asked pulling my hands to him.

"I'm good." I told him.

"I'm glad. It's crazy, I can't believe you even here right now." He laughed lowly.

"Kidnapping and robbery ain't funny. You could have at least given me some of the fucking money." I said rolling my eyes.

"You want some money baby?" he asked holding my hands again.

"Nah, you should probably save some money for your spouse." I replied mentioning his ex.

"The only thing I'm married to is the streets, I ain't on nothing else." He shrugged.

"I hear you," I nodded putting the menu up to my face.

"What you doing for the holidays?" he asked referencing the Christmas holiday that was quickly approaching.

Thinking about Christmas made me think about Justyce and thinking about Justyce made me think about his childish ass mama. She took him out of daycare claiming she couldn't afford it anymore. Well, that was the excuse she gave Ms. Dana, the owner of Busy Bee's daycare. Then anytime I called she refused to answer, but she would text me right back asking what I wanted. I wanted my nephew, not her. I didn't trust her with him at all. She in combination with her simple ass baby daddy had me frustrated. She just packed up her shit and left like it was okay or like it was normal. I talked a lot of shit but having Simone and Justyce in my life gave me purpose. Now, I didn't know what to do with myself which led me here accepting a date with a man I didn't really like just to get out of the house.

"Nothing, it seems. My sister moved out," I told him.

"Damn, she just dipped on you?" he asked.

"I mean we argued first, but yeah," I replied.

"You're more than welcome to come spend New Year's Eve with me. My dad always does this big ass party with all the dope boys and shit, you should come as my date," he told me.

"I don't even have anything super dressy to wear. It's formal, right?" I asked.

"Yeah, I'll pick the dress to match my Tux, all you gotta do is show up," he told me.

"Seems like you got this shit all planned out," I smiled.

"I gotta move fast when it comes to you Sinna, you ain't the easiest person to get to know," he said, rubbing my hands.

"I been through some shit. You're used to females to falling all over you cause of who you are, but I don't care about the hype, I want to get to know you as a person." I explained.

"I know, I can see that." he said staring at me.

"Okay," I nodded.

I let my eyes comb over the crowded restaurant before they landed on Saint sitting across from the female from our first encounter in his truck. He focused on me for a second or two longer before he rose from his seat and approached us.

"What up AJ?" Saint's deep voice demanded my attention.

"Sup Saint?" AJ spoke offering a slight head nod.

"Sup Sinna?" Saint asked as his eyes undressed me in my seat.

"Hey." I smiled back at him nervously.

I don't know what it was about Saint, but anytime he was around I was nervous and excited just at the sight of him.

"Saint, I ain't know you knew Sinna." AJ said looking from Saint and back to me.

"Yeah, me and shorty real cool." Saint smirked licking his lips.

"Saint is my best friend's cousin." I explained for AJ.

"How do you two know each other?" I asked watching them exchange glances.

"Saint works for me, baby." AJ spoke up.

"Nah, Saint works for yo daddy, nigga." Saint cleared it up.

Now, I understood the tension between them. As they continued their stare off Saint's girlfriend came over and introduced herself.

"Hi, I'm Erica." She offered to AJ who took her hand and shook it.

She glanced at me and frowned but didn't open her mouth again.

"I guess you two should be on your way." I smiled at Saint and his hoe.

Saint laughed and bent down brushing his lips against my ear.

"You cute, don't make me show my ass. Answer when I call." Saint told me and then walked away with his hoe right behind him.

He might as well had taken my soaked panties with him cause they were drenched now.

Surprisingly, AJ hadn't said anything about Saint whispering in my ear. I expected him to at least being in his feelings, but he wasn't, he was quiet though. After dinner at Applebee's, we ended up at the movie theater.

"Everything alright?" I asked him after we got out popcorn.

"Yeah, I'm cool. You?" he asked nonchalantly.

"Do you want to talk about it?" I pressed.

"Saint the reason you ain't really fucking with me, right?" he asked

It was so many ways I could answer that question, but I chose to be gentle with his feelings.

"I don't know why you keep saying that. I do fuck with you, but I'm not about to bend over backward trying to get your attention like one of them other bitches would. I been giving you a hard time cause you won't keep it real with me. I told you from the jump, I prefer honesty, you a young, fly nigga so I get it, you got hoes, you ain't gotta lie about that shit. I'm not your girl or your wife and I ain't trying to be." I explained to him.

"So, I ain't gotta worry about you and Saint?" he questioned me.

"All you should be worried about is these hoes finding out

you like cheap dates," I laughed and tossed a kernel of popcorn in my mouth.

"I just wanted to spend some time with you on a simple level. It ain't like we know that much about each other, you know?" he asked.

"Chill, I didn't know what you liked, and this little date is more than any of them hoes will ever get from me." He laughed.

"Tragic." I laughed just as he held the door open to the theater we were going on. During the movie, my phone kept ringing, so I finally got up and went to answer it in the hallway.

"Hey aunt—" my words were cut off by her words.

"SOMEBODY BROKE IN MY HOUSE!" she screamed.

My heart dropped. I didn't have any cash in the house or anything worth any value, but I knew she kept every dollar she ever made in her mattress.

"Oh my god!" I groaned. "Did—"

"It gotta be Simone! How else would anybody be able to break in and go right to my shit? They didn't touch shit else, don't even look like they were in your room at all!" she spat.

"Auntie, you don't—"

"I FUCKING KNOW! AND SO DO THE POLICE! YOU TELL YO HOE ASS SISTER THAT SHIT!" she screamed at me before the call ended.

"Everything alright?" AJ asked coming from behind me.

"I wish. Can you take me home?" I asked him.

"Of course, let's go," he told me leading me out of the movie theater.

When we pulled into the driveway a police car was still parked on the street.

"Thank you for tonight, I'm sorry about this, but I had a really good time and I can't wait to do it again. I'll call you," I told AJ as I reached for the door handle to get out the car.

"Text me all your sizes, so I can get your dress and shit for you," he told me grabbing my elbow before I could get out.

I nodded my head with a smile and then got out of the car and headed in the house. The front door had been kicked off the hinges and was now leaning against the frame. The picture frames that line the hallway had slashes through them and were now on the floor.

"Auntie?" I asked as I stood outside her door.

"Ma'am can we help you?" the officer from the police car asked approaching me from the back.

I turned around to face him and he quickly hovered a hand over his gun.

"Sinna, I hate that I even have to say this to you, but you gotta pack your stuff. You gotta go," she said refusing to look at me.

"I gotta go?" I asked as if I didn't understand what she said the first time.

I didn't actually understand what was going on. Why was she doing this to me? I didn't have anything to do with anybody breaking into her house, so why was she punishing me?

"I'm sorry Sinna, I don't know if maybe you got involved in some bullshit or what, but you can't stay here anymore. Ever since I let you two come live with me shit has been coming up missing, your sister been disrespectful to me and my house and I don't feel like either of you have done enough to get yourselves out of the situations your in. I gotta do what's best for me." She said explaining herself.

My mouth hung open for a second or two as I stared at her unsure of what to do next.

"Ma'am? Do you need to get some things for tonight?" the officer asked me touching my back lightly.

I snatched away from him and headed to my room to pack up some shit. I didn't know where to go or who I could talk to, so I packed all my clothes which was pretty much all that was left in the room except the queen size bed she let us sleep on. The two duffle bags I carried to the front door once I was finished packing felt like the weight of the world and technically it was, it was the weight of everything I owned.

"Do you need a ride somewhere ma'am?" the officer asked once I was walking through the front door.

"No, I can figure it out," I told him.

I'd already ordered an UBER before I came outside hoping by the time, I was finished my car would be outside and I could just hop in and head to a hotel for the night. Sure, I could have called Money or Khadija, but I didn't want to be saved, I got myself into this situation depending on my sister knowing she wouldn't do right all along. Speaking of my sister, I had some words for her ass.

"Hello?" she asked softly.

"You had that ain't shit nigga rob Auntie's house?" I asked her immediately.

"What?" she asked like she didn't hear me.

"You heard me," I repeated.

"I didn't have my nigga rob yo Auntie house!" she growled.

"Then you had some niggas do it then!" I accused her.

"You funny yo. Why would I do some dumb shit like that?" she asked.

"You know she put me out because of that shit, right?" I asked.

She was silent for a second.

"Damn, I'm sorry she did that shit. Why don't you go move in with one of yo little friends? I know Khadija will take you in, you love her," she hissed.

"Huh?" I frowned looking down at my phone.

"You fucking heard me! I always had yo back, I loved you Sinna. You did this, and you deserve everything you get!" she said crying.

"YOU NEVER HAD MY BACK! YOU NEVER LOVED ME!" I yelled at her.

"I was never mama's favorite, I was never anybody's favorite, not until I met Dirty. He ain't perfect, but he's mine. You don't like him, so you set him up with your girl? That's fucked up Sinna. I hate you! When you see me, don't speak just keep moving like we don't know each other because clearly we don't!" she said.

"Simone, I didn't set Khadija up with Dirty—"

The sound of the call ending interrupted my sentence.

"We're here ma'am," my driver told me once we reached the Microtel hotel.

After paying for the UBER and checking into the hotel for the night I sat on the double bed and cried. Not because of anything my Auntie said or even what Simone said. I was crying for me, I was tired. It seemed like no matter what I did or how hard I tried to do things the right way, nothing went the way it was supposed to. Apart of me wanted to call Khadija and ask her about what Simone was saying, but as I sat back and pieced conversations together between Simone and Khadija, I knew what she was saying was true. At least it looked like that from her perspective anyway.

Especially, when the nigga doing the dirt was probably in her ear filling her with lies to keep her away from me and anyone else that could have a positive pull on her. I was setting myself up for failure. Simone wasn't able to handle living on her own, why would I think that I would be any different than her?

I left the hotel room and walked across the street to the BP gas station. I didn't know what my plan was or what I planned to buy, but I felt like I needed something. I grabbed a bottle of water from the refrigerator and then headed to the counter.

"Let me get that bottle of Benadryl over there," I told the dude behind the counter.

He grabbed the liquid from behind him and scanned the medicine and then the water.

"I got her stuff. Let me get thirty on pump four too boss," a familiar voice said stepping in front of me.

I could only see the back of his head, but I knew those dreads anywhere.

"What are you doing here?" I asked watching him as he grabbed my stuff from the counter.

"Stopped to get gas," he shrugged.

"What you doing way over here on this side of town?" I quizzed as we walked outside.

"What you doing out here? You meeting somebody at the room?" he asked as he started pumping gas.

"No, I'm staying out here, you the one meeting one out hoes," I smirked.

"Nah, I'm fucking with you now. What's up with you?" he asked taking the bag from me and pulling my water out.

He opened the bottle and downed the entire bottle in a few gulps.

"Why did you drink all my water?" I pouted.

"I got a case of water right here," he said popping the trunk and handing me two. "Get in the truck, it's cold out here."

* * *

"What are you doing?" I asked when he got on the elevator with me.

"You think I give a fuck about AJ?" he asked stepping closer to me.

"You think I give a fuck about Erica?" I said, raising an eyebrow.

"Shut up and kiss me then." he said standing toe to toe with me.

I pushed my face closer to his, throwing my arms around

his neck and offered him a passionate kiss. Kissing wasn't something I did often, to me kissing was more intimate than sex, it was more personal. Being around Saint made me horny, but kissing Saint had me ready to pledge my allegiance to him. He took control, dominating our kiss leaving me dizzy with passion when the elevator doors opened, and he pulled away from our kiss. I led the way to my room where he barely let me open the door before, he was snatching my clothes off aggressively.

"Damn," he whispered as he stood in front of the bed.

I was lying on my back wearing only a bra while he only wore his boxer briefs. My eyes trailed down his body until they bugged out of my head watching him put the thin material of the condom over his dick. I'd only seen a dick with a curve in porn before. His length and girth had me a little intimidated, but I refused to show him that.

"You good?" he asked when he touched my leg and I jumped.

"Yeah," I nodded my head as I got comfortable on the bed.

"Come here," he demanded, pulling my body to him by my legs.

He put my legs in the crook of his arms and pushed his mushroom head against me.

"Ouch!" I jumped.

"You was talking all that shit and look at you, can't take a lil dick." Saint's deep voice called for my attention.

"Ain't nothing *little* about it." I told him rolling my eyes.

I looked up at him, focusing on his pretty face before his kiss distracted me and within seconds, he was inside of me. He was so deep it felt like he could scratch my head from the inside.

"Damn that shit tight," he moaned against my lips.

I loved the fact that he moaned, and kissed unlike most niggas, he kissed my lips, my neck, and chest as he snatched his thickness in and out of me. Saint pushed my legs over his shoulder and continued his assault, not caring that I had tears in my eyes or that he had me feeling so good I was seeing stars.

"Fuck!" I hissed.

"Shit feels good don't it, baby?" he asked before kissing me, not giving me a chance to reply.

"Tell me that shit then!" he demanded as he slammed his body against mine.

"You feel so fucking good." I moaned.

"Nah baby, we feel good. Look at that shit, you so fucking wet," he groaned as he continued delivering passionate strokes. "Ride my shit," he told me as he pulled me over on top of him.

I chose a slow, agonizing grind that had him whispering "God damn," repeatedly.

His hands found my clit which quickly had me bucking against his body as I rode him. His hands palmed my B cups briefly before he pulled my upper half down to him. He massaged my roots as he kissed me long and deep while he fucked me from the bottom. Every touch, kiss, and stroke from Saint was passionate and intentional. Just as I was on the verge of cummin' he stopped and snatched his condom covered dick out of me. He said nothing as he forced my body into a new position.

"Relax," he whispered as he pushed my upper back down into the bed.

A finger slipped inside of me momentarily before he snatched his finger away replacing it with his juicy lips. I held my breath and spread my legs wider as he kissed my pussy from the back. He pulled away briefly, turned over on his back and continued eating my pussy now that I was sitting on his face. I gripped his dreads as I rode his face, cummin' less than a minute later. He continued lapping at my juices making it hard for my weak body to pull away from him. Finally, he slid from underneath me and pushed himself inside of me as he held my limp body up. My mouth was dry, my voice was ragged, but my skin was soaked in sweat.

Not just my sweat, both his and mine mixed together covering both of our skin and the sheets. Each stroke he delivered resulted in the loud smacking sound Ms. Kitty made in applause as he destroyed her. Saint gripped my hips and as he pounded into me from behind.

"How many times I make you cum?" he asked before kissing my neck.

"Three—Three times." I panted.

His fingers found my clit easily and as he assaulted my clit with his thick middle finger his teeth sunk into my neck.

"Shit." He hissed leaning against me as we came together.

"Damn," he said laying down beside me.

I offered him a small smile and attempted to walk on wobbly legs to the bathroom.

"You good yo?" Saint asked holding back a laugh.

I closed and locked the bathroom door before making it to the toilet. No wonder that girl was acting a damn fool over his ass. I could tell by just looking at him that he had some good dick, but the shit he got going on needed to be copywritten. Even after I got in the shower, I could still feel him pounding inside me.

And he could polish the hell out of my clit with his devilish tongue. Yeah, he needed to stay far, far away from me with all of that. I couldn't afford to be dick drunk like Simone. After a shower, I stepped out of the bathroom expecting to see Saint sitting on the bed, but I was met with an empty room. I lay back on the bed, pulling a pillow over my face and screaming into it.

"You alright?" Saint asked scaring the shit out of me as he pulled the pillow back off my face.

"You scared me! Stop creeping up on me." I told him with a frown on my face.

"I ain't mean to scare you. I went down to get some extra clothes." He told me holding up a gym bag.

"You keep a hoe bag in your truck?" I asked stifling a laugh.

"Chill." He laughed with me for a second before his smile faded and that soul searching, intense glare he always gave me replaced it.

"Why you always look at me like that?" I asked nervously moving away from him.

"Benadryl ain't the answer." He said looking into my eyes.

"Neither is sex." I replied.

"Sex...is..." he was standing in front of me now.

He laughed when I jumped at his touched, he brushed the small group of dreads that swayed in my face and kissed my lips softly.

"Sex is natural." He kissed the side of my face.

His kiss trailed to the outside of my ear as he spoke.

"But sex with you? You fucked up giving me that shit, cause I ain't giving it back. That pussy belongs to me now." He hissed.

He brushed past me into the bathroom leaving me standing there in my towel trying to catch my breath. I found a pair of pajama pants and a tank top to sleep in before he stepped out of the bathroom wearing a pair of black basketball shorts and a black t-shirt.

"How did you know——"

"I don't know. I've been there before." He shrugged looking away from me.

The phone in his hand starting ringing with Khalifa's name on the display.

"What up?" he spoke into the phone.

He stood and moved out to the balcony to talk on the phone. I didn't mean to keep looking at him, but he kept walking back and forth and I couldn't help, but to watch him.

Finally, he stopped pacing with his back facing me. A few minutes later he turned around and came in.

"Why you staring at me?" he asked as he walked over to me.

"Your dreads are pretty, for a guy. Who does your hair?" I asked him.

"A chick I know." He offered.

"A chick you fucking does your hair, you really are a pimp out here." I laughed.

"So, any female that I know or talk to just gotta be fucking me?" he asked with an amused grin.

"Basically." I shrugged.

He laughed but used my hand to slid inside his basketball shorts and he used my hand to stroke his dick. I'd jacked a dick or two before but doing it with his hand on top of mine for some reason made it feel different. I climbed on top of him moving my hand out of the way, so I could feel his thick rod pressed against my pussy.

"Put it in." his voice was rough and raspy.

"You need a condom." I replied with a head shake.

"I'll pull out." He begged.

"No! you out here fucking off and shit." I declined as he used my body to grind against his dick.

His phone rang again interrupting him as he answered.

"Yo. Ain't I'm on my way." He said a few seconds later.

I hopped off his lap and sat down on the bed beside him.

"I wish I could kick it with you, but—"

"It's cool I wasn't expecting something serious." I helped him.

"Ima call you sometime tomorrow, aight?" he asked rubbing my thigh.

"Okay." I agreed.

I watched him walk out the door and rested my head on the soft pillow and drifted off to sleep.

5

———

KHADIJA

"Why are you on my phone?" I snapped as soon as I answered Dirty's phone call.

"What the fuck is wrong with you?" he asked matching my attitude.

"What's wrong with me? You go get one of yo baby mama's pregnant—"

"Aye, Khadija, I swear yo I only fucked her once," he lied.

"You only fucked her once?" Tears filled my eyes as I shook my head.

I wanted to believe him, but he'd lied to me too many times. Dirty was exactly what his childhood nickname implied, *dirty*. He was all about a dollar, if it didn't make him money, then he had an issue with it. After I made it clear that I wasn't paying for dick our relationship settled into a friendship. Well, a sexuationship which I was cool with, he is the one that wanted a relationship, he is the one that didn't want me talking to anybody else. And like a dumb ass I agreed and look at me, almost two years later, always fighting him and his baby mama's for his attention.

Of course, it wasn't always like this. When we first started fucking around, I didn't tell anybody and then I kept the secret because, I didn't want to hear the backlash behind it. Of course, my family knew, but Money and Sinna didn't, I mean they knew *Derrick* because that's how I referred to him. I called myself protection my relationship when really all I was doing was helping him hide what we were doing.

"Khadija, baby I'm sorry," he mumbled the familiar phrase lowly.

"Then stop doing shit to be sorry for!" I screamed into the phone.

"We gotta talk about this shit face to face," he replied.

"Don't even try to come over here," I said rolling my eyes.

"Damn, I can't come see you? It's like that?" he asked sounding hurt.

"Khalifa is here," I told him.

"This is between me and you, why you always trying to bring yo brother in our shit?" he asked.

"I'm not, I'm just telling you, he's here." I shrugged as if he could see me.

"Well, I'm just trying to talk to you, we ain't gone be loud or fuss or nothing.

He said that now, but once he was here and Khalifa was in his shit, he would be ready to leave. Plus, I knew if I talked to him face to face then I would fall for his bullshit after his first round of apologies.

"Saint and Kidd here too and—"

"Oh, yo little boyfriend there, so you don't want me to come over?" he asked.

"Are you serious right now?"

"Dead fucking serious," he replied.

"You know what? You right, Kidd my nigga now," I laughed.

"Oh, that shit funny?" he asked sounding upset.

"As hell. Imagine how I feel with everybody on social media knowing about your fuck sessions with yo baby mama? We're both fucking pregnant Derrick!" I yelled at him.

"Bae, I promise you it's been a minute since I fucked Simone—"

"So, it's true, that's your baby mama? After all this time this is how I find out who she is?" I asked.

"Khadija, please just give me five minutes to explain please baby," he begged.

"No, Derrick. You said it was all about us and then you turn around and get her pregnant. You knew she was Sinna's sister, you could have said something at any time. You could have prevented all this shit. I'm not fucking with you no more. Don't come to my house, don't come to my job and don't fucking call me no more." I snapped before I hung up the phone.

Sure, while Khalifa and Saint were going through "daddy boot camp" with my dad in Atlanta, Kidd and I got close. We were friends though, nothing more than that. He was a good listener and he kept it real with me. But other than a close friendship nothing happened. Well, one night we almost fucked, he stopped though. He said he couldn't let it happen out of respect for Khalifa. He was a hoe just like Saint and Khalifa, so as bad as I wanted to fuck him, he just didn't make me feel special. What I had with Kidd was more than just sex.

Since Dirty wanted to bring up Kidd, I was going to spend some time with him just to piss him off. I stormed out of my bedroom and stopped in the living room looking for Kidd, but he wasn't sitting in there playing the game with Khalifa and Saint.

"Where's Kidd?" I asked.

"He went to play ball," Saint replied.

"Fuck you want to know for?" Khalifa asked grilling me.

I ignored Khalifa and headed down to the basketball goal

around the corner. I watched Khalifa shooting the ball around by himself for a few minutes before I walked over to him and waited for him to address me.

"Wassup?" he asked.

"You miss it don't you?" I asked him.

"What basketball? Yeah, I miss being out here shaking niggas up," he laughed bouncing the basketball between my legs and spinning around me before shooting a basket.

"So, why not go after that?" I asked him.

"Nah, shit was a whole lifetime ago. I'm good," he shrugged, shooting another basket.

"How come you never taught me how to play?" I asked.

"You never asked. I guess you were scared to break a nail or some shit," he smirked.

"Whatever teach me how to play," I whined.

He laughed and tossed the ball my way. I gave a slight effort to reach for the ball, but it bounced away from me.

"What you doing? You gotta actually try to get the ball Khadija," Kidd scolded me as he jogged over to get the ball.

"I did try, you threw it too hard," I lied.

"What you come down here for?" he asked now holding the ball on his hip as he stood in front of me.

"Cause you ain't been talking to me and I wanted to check on you," I replied.

"Nah, cause you think I'm mad at you," he called me out.

"Saint told you?" I asked in disbelief.

"You thought he was gone keep something like that a secret?" Kidd asked squinting at me.

"I didn't think you were going to be mad, disappointed that I wasn't using protection—"

"Wait, what?" he cut me off with a confused look on his face.

"YOU PREGNANT?" he blurted out.

"You said Saint told you!" I yelled in shock.

"That nigga ain't tell me shit! You let that nigga get you pregnant?" he asked in disbelief.

I dropped my head allowing my eyes to focus on the ground too embarrassed to speak.

"I know Khalifa don't know yet. What the fuck you doing yo?" he asked.

"You act like I intentionally got pregnant." I shrugged.

"You damn sure didn't intentionally *not* get pregnant." He spat.

"Kidd, I could really use a friend right now." I spoke honestly.

"Yo, I'ma always look out for you, I'm always gon want you to win, but I ain't fucking with you like that no more. I was there for you, let you cry on my fucking shoulder when that nigga was out here treating you like shit then you go right back to him. You just forget all about me and I'm the one that built you up after he knocked you down!" he barked in my face.

"Kidd, that's not true!" I spat with tears in my eyes.

"So, I'm fucking crazy or I'm just a fucking liar?" he growled at me.

"No, but you're my brother's friend and you was the one worried about what Khalifa was going to say about me and you fucking around," I reminded him.

"Right about me and you fucking around, but I told you if you were serious, then I was down. You stopped fucking calling me and a week later you and that nigga back on y'all shit. That's how you do me," he recalled.

He was right. Dirty, had some kind of spell on me. It didn't matter what was going on or who was a part of it, it seemed like all he had to do was snap his fingers and I'd come running. I hated that I was weak for him, but I loved him so much, his happiness was starting to mean more to me than my own. I knew it, I could feel it happening, but I couldn't do anything to stop it.

"You can't help who you love," I stated weakly.

"Love ain't pain. You realize it's two different words, right?" he asked mugging me.

"Trey—"

"Nah, I'm good yo. You and yo baby daddy enjoy yo life," he told me pushing past me.

"TREY!" I yelled his name just before he walked out of the fence that surrounded the basketball court.

He turned around and looked at me giving me a look that said I was getting on his fucking nerves.

"Please don't tell Khalifa," I called out to him.

He laughed and then took off running. My heart dropped for a second or two while I watched him get closer to my house. I took off running after him, I knew I would never catch up to him due to his athletic background, but at least I'd make it to the house in time to catch Khalifa before he stormed out of the house headed to kill Dirty. By the time I made it to my house I was out of breath and barely able to speak, but my legs didn't stop moving until I was standing outside the back door, holding the doorknob as I tried to catch my breath in the cold weather.

"OH, I'MA KILL THAT NIGGA!" Khalifa's loud voice vibrated through the door.

I snatched my hand off the door like it was on fire and stepped back, giving him room to step out.

"HERE YOU GO! What's wrong with you?" Khalifa asked with a face full of disappointment.

"Ain't nothing wrong with me! I made a mistake, don't make it seem like you ain't never slipped up and gave a bitch a couple hundred to take care of it," I accused him.

"That's where you got me fucked up! I don't fuck nothing raw, you don't know what that nigga out here doing! You walking around here all sad and shit with yo head down and now you bringing a baby in the world. You working at

Wendy's, that ain't enough to take care of you, how you gone take care of a baby?" Khalifa went off on me.

"I'm not gone be doing it alone, first of all!" I yelled at him.

By this time, Saint and Kidd were both outside standing around watching the argument unfold as usual.

"And you can wipe that stupid ass smirk off yo fucking face!" I pushed a finger into Kidd's face.

"Go head," he laughed at my antics, but I had something for him since he felt the situation was funny.

"I almost slept with Kidd too, since he broadcasting what's happening between my legs," I said folding my arms across my chest.

"Chill yo," Kidd said, shaking his head now that Saint and Khalifa were focused on him.

"Nah, you should keep yo fucking mouth closed!" I yelled at him.

"I fuck with you, but respect how you speak to me shorty." he said, furrowing his eyes at me.

"I said what I said! Khalifa, you can feel however you want about Dirty, but he's my child's father and he's going to be in his child's life!" I spat defiantly.

"Only, if I miss," Khalifa told me.

"What are y'all out here arguing about now?" my mama asked stepping outside holding her back.

"Go head, tell her!" Khalifa spat grilling me.

"Khalifa!" I groaned stomping my feet.

"Look at you! You a grown-ass woman, right? You can't even tell yo mama she about to be a grandma." He rubbed it in.

"What? No, Khadija." My mama shook her head as she looked at me waiting for me to deny what he said, but I couldn't.

"I'm sorry." I said feeling like a little ass kid.

"Ain't no need to be sorry now, shit the deed is done. Come in here and talk to me. Khalifa, stop cussing in my damn house, y'all boys go get me a soda please." She blew them off like it took more than one of them to go around the corner for her.

"I ain't gone miss, Khadija." Khalifa told me storming off with Kidd and Saint following in his footsteps to his car before he burned rubber pulling off.

SINNA

SINNA

After all the drama with Simone and my aunt, I pushed all their bullshit aside and focused on myself. I finally passed my GED test and barely squeezed in enough time to register for some college classes. I only ended up spending a few days in the hotel before Money came over and forced me to move in with her. Living with Money was actually pretty cool, she was considerate and funny. She didn't want me to help her pay half the bills, but I planned to even if she didn't believe that I would. She was mostly never home which made me feel like a bum for not having a second job when she was constantly working or out doing something. It wasn't much that I could do about feeling like a bum, so I kept her house clean, I cooked, and I bought food items to help out since I was still working part-time.

Finally, it was New Year's Eve and AJ was taking me to some formal party that his family held for the street niggas every year, and I was actually excited to see him again. Since I'd been focused on school and work, I hadn't seen him other than a few facetime calls here and there, but we talked pretty frequently. He was funny, sexy, and just the right amount of thug to keep me interested. He was entertaining, but nothing compared to the time I spent with Saint.

Saint was…*everything*.

But after that night, his conversation was hit and miss. He would call or text during the day, but we only saw each other once or twice since he fucked me. I wanted more of him, I wanted all his attention, but he seemed distracted to say the least. Unlike AJ who was consistent in his phone calls and text messages.

"What you call me over here for?" Khadija asked as she came through the door with Money on her heels.

"Cause we ain't seen you in a minute hoe." I joked with her.

Ever since the drama with Simone happened Khadija had been standoffish and extremely short with me. Our relationship was awkward now and I hated it, but I didn't know what to say to her or how to fix the crack in our relationship.

"I know, I been busy trying to work two jobs and juggle this baby shit. A bitch is tied, boss." She said sitting down on the sectional.

"I know you are, I can only imagine what you're going through. I wish things were better for you," I replied.

"Thank you," she smiled at me.

"Can we talk about the reason I asked everyone here?" Money said dramatically.

"Hurry up, I got shit to do after this," I joked.

"So, the past few weeks I been trying out a few things and I got an idea that's gone make us a shit ton of money," Money replied looking from Khadija to me.

"Long as I ain't gotta sell my ass, I'm down. It's hard out here for a pimp," Khadija replied making us laugh.

"Nah, it ain't selling ass, it's credit card scamming," she shrugged like the shit she was saying was normal, okay and legal.

"Credit cards? That shit sounds like a prison sentence," I said shaking my head no.

"It's a foolproof plan. I got a plug to the credit card numbers, I already bought a shit ton of blank credit cards that we gone press them with the numbers and then we gone go buy whatever the fuck we want," she spat.

"That shit sound crazy," I shook my head violently.

"It ain't, it's simple and it put five grand in my bank account this week," she said with a playful eye roll.

"Let me hold something then," I asked extending my hand.

She dropped a credit card in my hand and smirked at me.

"Who the hell is Aileene Moreno?" I asked looking at her.

"It's the bitch that's going to get a cash advance, so she can put a down payment down on a car or shit load of baby clothes," she said looking at Khadija as she dropped a card in her hand.

"What if we get caught?" I asked her.

"What if you sitting on the front porch and an officer catches you smoking weed?"

"You'd get a citation and the shit would be over," she shrugged.

"I'm not sold," I shook my head no.

"You can always sell yo ass," Khadija smirked.

"Go head." I said pushing her playfully.

"What y'all doing tonight?" Khadija asked. "We should watch scary movies and eat popcorn and shit—"

"I can't, I got a date," I said looking away.

"A date? With who?" Money asked.

"AJ invited me to some party his dad—"

"Bitch, you partying with all the hustlers tonight then," Money said with a smirk.

"I guess, I'm just going because he claims he talked to his dad about me and wants us to meet," I said rolling my eyes.

"That's sweet Sinna," Khadija said bumping me.

"I guess. I haven't decided how I feel about him yet," I told them.

"Why not? He seems pretty serious about you," Money replied.

"We'll see how long he lasts. They all seem serious in the beginning," I said with a slight eye roll.

* * *

"Damn, you looking good baby," AJ complimented me when he came to pick me up later that night.

"Thank you." I offered him a smile.

I was wearing an off the shoulder all-white dress that fit my body perfectly. AJ was wearing an all-black Tux, his jewelry shined brightly under the dim lighting.

"Okay, I see y'all. Y'all should take a picture for the gram," Money said with her phone in her hand.

"It's cool," I attempted to stop her, but AJ wouldn't let me.

"Nah, let her take the picture baby," he told me.

He made sure to push our bodies together and rest his hand on my ass while Money took the picture.

"You should put that one on your page AJ," Money said with a sly grin.

"Don't you have a date or two to go on?" I asked with a laugh.

"That's funny to you?" AJ asked with a straight face.

"I'm just saying, you ain't gotta put me on your IG, you know I don't like social media like that." I tried to explain, but he wasn't having it.

"Send me the picture after she sends it to you. Matter of fact Money just inbox it to me on IG," he told her ignoring me like I wasn't there at all.

After he finally got the picture, posted it on IG, and tagged me in it, I started getting new followers out of nowhere. We drove for a minute before we were stopping in a long ass line of cars leading to a driveway. The driveway was so long we couldn't see the house from where we were making a slow roll to the front of the line.

"Damn, it's a lot of people here." I mumbled starting to feel nervous.

"It's okay, stay close to me and you'll be fine." He said rubbing my knee and throwing me a wink.

After AJ spoke to the guard about football, we were on our way moving towards the massive house with what could have easily been hundreds of luxury cars everywhere. People were crawling all over the place and suddenly I felt out of place.

"You good?" he asked holding my hand.

"Why is it so many people here?" I asked looking around.

"It's the New Year niggas wanna party and get drunk to end the year." he shrugged.

"Come on girl." He demanded climbing out the car and then reaching back for me.

I hesitantly grabbed his hand and followed him out of the car. He led me around the property speaking to people I'd never seen before and probably would never see again. We danced, ate a bunch of fancy shit I can't repeat or explain before AJ dragged me out to the balcony area.

"You enjoying yourself?" AJ whispered in my ear later on as he held me close to him.

"I've been looking for you all night. Hi Sinna. I need to borrow AJ for a minute." Ms. Dana said offering a wide smile.

"You look very nice Ms. Dana." I told her as I accepted her one arm hug.

"Where's dad?" AJ asked her.

"He's in his office, he's asking for you." She smiled.

"Okay, I'll be back baby." AJ said kissing my jaw before he disappeared.

"You enjoying yourself Sinna?" Mrs. Dana with a smile.

"I am. Although, I got to admit I don't know anybody here." I spoke honestly.

"Nothing wrong with that. How's Justyce doing?" she probed.

"He's good. I saw him on Christmas. I miss him so much." I revealed.

"I miss him too. All you can do is pray for your sister though. Sometimes people have to go through things on their own." She shrugged as she sipped her champagne.

"Where yo husband?"

The man that interrupted our conversation towered over Ms. Dana and my short five-feet four or so inch frames. He was a dark brown complexion with long, dark all-black locs that hung down his back stopping at his waist, his face formed a deep scowl as his eyes rested on Ms. Dana. Ms. Dana's body bent closer to him instantly, her eyes bore into him and he stared right back down at her both of them lost in the moment. He glanced at me and his jaw dropped as recognition covered his face.

He knew me!

Ms. Dana must have realized at this point that I was still standing here cause she cleared her throat and turned around to face me.

"They all went to his office." She spoke looking back at him, but he was staring at me.

The way he looked at me sent chills through me.

How did he know me?

"Fletch, this is AJ's girlfriend—"

"Sinna." He finished her sentence for her as we stared at each other.

"How do you—"

"I'm Fletch." He said as he stared at me.

"Do I know you from somewhere?" I asked since he seemed to be staring at me like he knew me.

"I knew your mama." He replied still focused on me.

"You knew my mom?" I repeated his question as I looked up at him.

"I don't think anybody could forget Ana Jackson." He offered a small smile my way.

"Yeah, I bet." I replied feeling a tinge of embarrassment.

My mama wasn't exactly the head of the PTO if you know what I mean. She was a crackhead, but not the type to hide from the people she knew. She begged, borrowed, and stole from people that knew her from her normal life so, his statement resonated with me.

"I loved her." He pushed out grabbing my attention.

My eyes roamed over his deep caramel complexion looking for anything that resembled me. His deep-set almond-shaped eyes matched mine, our lips were the same, even down to the way he was holding his mouth matched mine.

"Are you my…" my words trailed off.

I couldn't bring myself to ask the question. Over the years I imagined what my father looked like. I'd dreamt of him constantly as a child, hoping and praying that one day he would come and rescue me. It wasn't like I was missing something cause most of the kids I went to school with didn't have fathers either, but that didn't stop the need that ached inside of me. And now I was standing in front of a man who claimed to love my mom and who looked so much like me. I was so afraid of his response to being my father I couldn't even say the words.

What if I asked and he said no?

"I don't know for sure—"

He was saying something, but I took off running away from him before I could hear the rest of what he was going to say. My feet kept moving until I couldn't run anymore, my chest burned with each breath I attempted to squeeze into my lungs until I let out a long sob. I couldn't believe it, I was right he was my father, he was right here in Raleigh in the same place I was in. Where had he been all this time?

"Sinna? You good?"

How was he always around when I was going through something?

"What do you want?" I asked turning around to face Saint.

His hand reached for my face and I backed away just as he was about to touch me.

"What are you doing?" I asked with a frown.

"You're crying. What's wrong? AJ did something to you?" He asked standing so close to me I could smell the Winter fresh gum in his mouth.

I shook my head no, still unable to speak.

"What's up? Why you crying then?" He asked.

"Fuck that meeting, come here." Saint replied yanking me into a small storage area behind a door.

"Get off me!" I pushed against him.

He didn't bulge, but he did grab my wrists tightly.

"I don't put my hands on women so don't put yo hands on me. Now, did someone hurt you?" he asked searching my eyes.

I shook my head no slowly.

"Don't cry shorty, I got you." He told me backing me against the wall.

He locked the door and devoured my lips and tongue giving me no space to breathe much less stop him, not that I wanted to. I held out while he kissed me, but once his hands lifted my dress above my hips, I couldn't hold back any longer. His fingers trespassed into my panties and inside of me without any issues. I threw my head back and closed my eyes tight as his fingers brought me on the brink of ecstasy. His pants hit the floor and seconds later he had my legs in the crook of both arms as he used the wall for leverage as he pounded me.

"You give that nigga my pussy?"

"This ain't yo pussy." I told him.

His pumps stopped instantly and motioned for me to be quiet for a second or two. I strained my ears to find out what he was hearing.

"You hear that?" he asked.

"What?" I asked with an attitude.

"She said she belong to me." He snatched out of my pussy and she replied with a loud smacking sound.

"That pussy belong to me, you hear me?" his full lips covered mine as he slammed into me.

"I hear you." I moaned against his lips.

He continued stroking me until we both came loud muffling our moans with kisses.

"Damn, that was good." I said feeling the high of my orgasm.

"Hell yeah, it was good. I miss you." Saint said as I stepped out of my thong.

I opened my mouth to speak, but he stopped me.

"I know it's my fault and shit, but I miss you." He told me.

"Saint, I'm not playing this game with you. I'm dating AJ now." I told him.

Saint walked over to me, grabbed my hand taking my thongs from me and put them in his pants.

"Fuck AJ." He replied.

"Did you *not* just hear me say I'm dating AJ?" I asked him.

"You can date whoever you want, long as we clear on who you fucking." He replied.

"Can I have my panties back please?" I asked with my palm open for him.

"In the morning. Let's go" He flashed me a smile as he headed to the door.

"What is Erica gone think when her date up and leaves without her?" I asked him.

"I ain't her date, she saw me and glued herself to my damn hip. The question is what are you going to tell AJ?" he asked raising an eyebrow at me as he spoke.

6

SAINT

After sneaking out of the party with Sinna we went to her house to pick up some clothes for her to spend the night. I fucked with Sinna cause she was different than any female I'd ever fucked with before. She was pretty as hell, but she was down to earth and ghetto too, and for some reason, that combo was stuck in my head. I could hear Sinna on the phone as she moved around her room and I knew it was AJ on the other end. She was grinning and smiling into the phone like she was alone, and that shit was pissing me off. I knew I couldn't really be upset cause I was still playing with fire fucking with Erica unstable ass.

"I'm not sure what I'm doing tomorrow." Sinna giggled into the phone interrupting my snooping through her panty drawer.

"Boy! I'll call you tomorrow," she lied as she rolled her eyes as she glanced at me.

I knew she was lying cause she wasn't going home tomorrow night. After the session we had in the storage at AJ's peoples' house I was trying to climb up in that motherfucka and stay. It was New Year's Eve, it was quickly approaching midnight and my pussy was being held hostage by Sinna's ole mean ass.

"Why you ain't tell me you passed yo GED test, Sinna?" I demanded to know as I eyed her.

"I hadn't really had a chance to talk to you, you know." She pointed out.

"You could have texted me or called and told me during any of our conversations since then." I stated.

"I didn't think it was that big of a deal." She shrugged.

"It's a big ass deal Sinna!" I told her.

"You gone punish me for not listening?" she grinned biting down on her bottom lip.

"Come on. I demanded.

Once we made it to my apartment, she used my bathroom to shower and I used the guest bathroom. I finished first and was laying across the bed with a frown plastered on my face.

"What's wrong with you?" she asked looking pretty as fuck.

A white towel played peek-a-boo giving me an eyeful while she struggled to keep it wrapped around her completely.

"Waiting on my pussy, come on you already making me late," I told her pulling her down on the bed with me.

"Late? What the hell are you talking about?" she asked relaxing in my embrace.

"I wanted to bring my New Year in buried deep inside you, but you rather spend your time doing a bunch of shit that don't matter" I told her my plans.

"Look, if we gone be fucking then let's just do that, but you can't just disappear until you get ready to fuck with me again and then order me around. We need to lay some ground rules and—"

Her trying to put her foot down with me was cute, but none of that shit was gone fly for me. I did whatever the fuck I wanted, and it wasn't a soul on Earth that was gone tell me otherwise. Her words were interrupted by the kiss I planted on her lips as I gripped her ass, keeping our bodies pressed tightly together.

She didn't pull away until my right hand slid under her towel, grazing her bare ass. The loud ringing of my cell phone made her push me away. I glanced at the display and groaned silently seeing Erica's name.

"Answer it, I'll make us something quick to eat." Sinna told me kissing my lips and disappearing out of my bedroom.

I stepped into a pair of sweats and stepped out of my apartment to answer the phone.

"Aye, my fault yo." I started talking to Erica.

"You could have given me a head-up if you were leaving, Saint." She scolded me.

"I said my fault, but I really don't even owe you that. You didn't come with me." I spat.

"I'm having your baby!" she barked.

"Man, you pregnant, but we don't know who that baby belongs to." I replied.

"I need you, Saint." She replied.

"Look, I already told you, I'll be here until the baby is born and we get a DNA test." I told her again.

"I thought we were better than that." She hissed.

"And I thought you were on birth control." I replied.

She hung up the phone in my face making me laugh. I lit the blunt I'd been rolling while I spoke to Erica and sat on the stairs while I smoked. I didn't know what I was going to do about Erica and this baby situation. I really didn't want Erica to have my baby, but I knew I'd been fucking her raw, so I knew I had to step up, but that ain't mean I had to be happy about it.

"Are you supposed to be smoking in here?" Sinna's soft and sweet voice carried over to me from where she stood.

She was wearing one of my t-shirts over her slim thick frame outlining all her curves.

"Come here. Come talk to me, baby." I urged her with a head nod.

She walked over to me and I wrapped my arms around her as I looked down at her.

"You gone fuck me out here in the stairwell?" she asked looking up with dreamy eyes.

"Girl, I'd fuck yo pretty ass anywhere," I told her honestly.

"That's all you want to do," she said pushing me back.

"I like fucking you, what's wrong with that? I don't remember you complaining either time," I laughed.

"Whatever," she said trying to walk away.

I grabbed a handful of asses once she turned around.

"You so mannish," she laughed.

"You like that shit though."

When we went back into my apartment Sinna walked around my apartment touching shit and learning about me. I ate the eggs, bacon, and toast sandwich she made as I watched her. She paused as she stood in front of my GED certificate while she held it in her hand.

"You ever take the test?" I asked her.

"Yeah, I'm registered for a few classes this semester." She replied.

"For real? I'm proud of you." I told her with a head nod.

"Thank you." She grinned.

"Do my hair for me." I spoke up.

"Oh, shit you want me to give you pussy and do your hair? Aw, shit I'm moving up." She laughed.

"You realize you still ain't said Happy New Year yet?" I asked her.

"Happy New year." She grinned as she melted in my arms.

* * *

The next day we went back to her place, so she could do my hair. She stepped out in the hallway to talk to Money and while she was running her mouth I was taking in her space. I noticed a teal-colored board behind an erasable calendar that was marked with different colors on different dates. Her bed was made perfectly with several colorful decorative pillows lined across the top of it. At the foot of the bed was a note-book with a list of shit on it, I picked it up and saw it was a wish list.

"You nosy as hell, you know that?" she asked snatching the notebook out of my hands and folding it over.

"Damn, I can't even see what you working on?" I asked with a smile.

"I'ma jump in the shower, so you can make yourself at home," she told me before she walked out of the room.

I looked around the well-decorated room and tried to find something else to focus on, but my mind went back to the notebook I found, so I picked it back up and went through it. The page it was on was a to-do list, but the rest of the book was a journal. I continued flipping through until I saw my name grace the pages. This journal entry was recent from the first night we had sex. I heard the shower go off on the other side of the bedroom door, so I knew I didn't have that much time, but after reading the shit I just read, I didn't give a fuck if she caught me or not.

"Give me my notebook!" Sinna sounded off the second she was completely in the room.

"Nah yo, tell me this shit ain't real. Tell me this shit right here ain't true," I told her as she attempted to snatch the book out my hands.

"It's none of yo fucking business!" she replied.

"Nah, you gone have to give me more than that," I shook my head.

She moved around the room basically ignore me, but I

wasn't letting up. The page I was on was filled with sadness, she was hopeless, and silently screaming for help.

"How I save you?" I asked.

She continued to ignore me while she squeezed a decent amount of lotion on her hands and began working it into her legs. I watched her move the towel back, exposing her pretty caramel thigh.

"Aye, yo, I asked you a question," I said getting upset.

She moved the towel off her body and reached for the lotion bottle again just as I smacked the lotion down to the floor.

"Why would you do that shit?" she snapped jumping to her feet.

"You gone answer me now?" I asked staring into her eyes.

"What you want me to say? You read it!" she yelled at me.

"You still feel like that?" I asked her.

"Are we fucking or not?" she asked walking towards me and grabbing my dick.

I grabbed her hand and she tried to snatch it away from me, but I used my free hand to grab her by her chin. With both her hands-free she swung at me trying to pull away from me, but my grip was too tight.

"I asked you a question," I growled.

"Get off me!" she said trying to shake away from me.

"Fuck you wanna kill yo self for?" I whispered letting her win the tug of war we were playing over her face.

"WHY NOT?" she screamed.

I pushed her body over to the mirror that was stuck to the door in the closet. I leaned my body on the wall beside the door facing her while she focused on the floor to avoid my eye contact.

"Sinna, look at you."

She closed her eyes and shook her head no. I saw the discolored marks on her upper thigh and hip area.

"You're beautiful.

Her eyes looked down at the obvious trauma on her leg. I dropped down to my knees and gave her several light kisses up and down her leg while I gripped an ass cheek.

"I ain't got shit," she said.

"Me either," I shrugged.

She rolled her eyes.

"I ain't gone ever have shit," she told me.

"Oh, nah you on yo own in that, cause I'ma get this money. I might not be the richest nigga, but I'ma have everything I need," I told her.

"Can you just fuck me now?" she asked huffed.

I grabbed her naked body and pushed her onto the bed. I took off my shirt and my jeans as I got back to bed.

"Face down, ass up," I told her as I snatched my boxer briefs off.

"Like this?" she asked pushing her ass towards the ceiling.

I stroked my dick slowly as I stood behind her, I gave her ass a smack and watched the ripple effect across her cheeks.

"Damn," I groaned.

Sinna was more on the slim thick side, but her shit jiggled when she walked and damn sure when I smacked it. I felt how hot her pussy was as I pushed against her body trailing kisses down her back, stopping at her ass. I planted kisses on her cheeks and kissed her pussy lightly making her jump. I slipped my tongue inside her as I covered her pussy with my mouth.

"Shit, Saint," she panted as she tried to getaway.

"Fuck you running for? Bring my pussy here," I demanded pulling her back towards me.

"Just fuck me," she replied.

"Aight," I grabbed her by her waist and shoved my dick inside her.

"Oh, fuck!" she cried out as she tried to get away from me.

I gripped her hips and pounded into her.

"Take that shit! You don't want to talk to me, you want to fuck me, right?" I asked as I punished her.

"You talk too fucking much!" she spat looking over her shoulder at me.

I snatched my dick out of her and pushed her over to her back quickly. She tried to push me off her, but I pushed her hands down and pushed inside of her, not giving her a chance to stop me.

"Talk that shit now," I growled.

"Pull out a little bit," she pleaded, pushing me back with one hand.

I smacked her hand off me.

"Nah, you were talking shit. What's up?" I asked staring down into her eyes.

"I'm finna cum," she moaned.

I was talking shit, but fucking Sinna without a condom had me ready to bust quick as hell. She was soaking wet and her pussy had me locked in place.

"Buss in my mouth," I demanded as I snatched out of her and replaced my dick with my lips and tongue.

Her body shook as she came, gripping my dreads with her hands, and gripping my face with her thighs.

"I don't know what you got going on, and if you don't want to talk then I respect that," I told her as I kissed up her body.

Her body jumped, and she moaned under my soft touches and light kisses.

"But that pussy needs me just as much as I need her. You see how she be crying for me?" I asked as I hovered over her damp body.

She nodded her head yes as she looked up at me. Her hands rested on the sides of my face and I kissed her palms gently.

"If you ain't got nobody to talk you out the stupid shit, then think about me. How deep I be in my pussy," I told her as I gripped her legs and held them in the crook of my arms. "You remember how you feel when I'm making my pussy cry."

I replied.

I dove back inside her and instead of beating it up, I slowed my strokes down and wound my hips, leaving no space between our bodies.

"You feel me, baby?" I asked, seeing the drunk look in her eyes.

She nodded her head yes.

"Nah, I need to hear you say that shit," I said not backing down.

"Saint, please!" she cried out.

I focused on her face as I lay on top of her with her legs on my shoulders, her hands in my dreads and my arms wrapped around her as our bodies slid over and over on top of each other.

"Say the words baby," I moaned against her lips.

"I won't kill myself," she finally told me.

Seconds later our juices mixed together, and I didn't give a fuck about pulling out. Sinna wasn't the first girl I'd nutted in, but she was the first girl I ever nutted in that had me on some*what happens just happens* type shit.

"Why do you care if I die or not?" she asked me once we both caught our breath.

"Nobody should feel like that," I told her.

Growing up I never had shit, the bitch that half-ass raised me was a dope fiend and my daddy probably was one of the many she used to stay high. She stayed clean off and on up until I was ten, then she was mostly high.

Those times were the worst.

I wasn't the kid that got budget-friendly shoes at the beginning of the school year, I wasn't the kid that got hand me downs. Most of my shit came from the Salvation Army or Khalifa and Khadija's mama, Nikki. Aunt Nikki was young enough to understand how it felt to be a kid but old enough to whoop yo ass old school grandma style. She worked two jobs as a nursing assistant from eleven at night to seven in the morning and then she worked eight to four at a group home. She did what she could for me growing up, and I appreciated the fuck out of her for that cause without her, I wouldn't have had shit.

Living in the hood meant kids counted gunshots instead of sheep to fall asleep, trash lined the sidewalks and gutters, and corner stores slowly changed hands from black mom and pop owned stores to those owned by foreigners. Where crackheads lived in abandoned houses just to steal all the copper to buy more of the same drug that kept them on the streets. Growing up in McDougald Terrace projects was hell, but at the same time, it was home. I ain't have shit, my neighbors ain't have shit, the only motherfuckas that had something was the dope boys that was putting in work. I looked up to them niggas, couldn't wait to be old enough to sell dope, that's all I ever wanted to do. Everybody loved and respected them, niggas, women wanted to fuck 'em, hell even my mama loved the dope boys.

The two-bedroom apartment we had quickly became a dope house. She met Ace and he offered to "take care of her" in exchange for using her apartment. Less than a year later she was completely turned out, Ace was ready to leave her by then, he was tired of her stealing his product, so he left one night after he threatened to kill her and told me to come to work when I was ready.

"Mommy, you okay?" I asked her a few weeks later.

She ignored me and walked over to the window scratching her arms. She'd sold damn near everything in the apartment in exchange for a hit. I wrapped my arms around her waist and she shook me off, pushing me down to the floor.

"Get the fuck off me! It's your fault he left!" she screamed at me.

"Mommy, please stop," I begged her as she kicked me repeatedly.

For a woman that was barely five feet and a hundred pounds soaking wet, she was strong as hell. She snatched me from the floor by my baby afro, tearing hair from the root as she dragged me across the room. She opened the front door and tried to push me out of the apartment as I screamed, kicked and held onto the door and the frame with all my strength. My fingernails dug in the wooden door and the paneling as I held on like my life depended on it.

I was almost ten around this time, and I'd just started skipping school. I didn't know what the fuck they were doing in class, I was a class clown. I'd been held back a grade, and I was constantly suspended from school for fighting. After the incident with my mama I missed a week of school, the school called my aunt Nikki since she was the one listed on my emergency contact information. The day she came over to check on me was the fourth day my mama spent starving me while she tricked for her "medicine" in her bedroom.

"Janay, open this god damn door!" my aunt Nikki demanded.

Her voice was direct, with no hint of playfulness. This wasn't a social visit, she meant business.

"Nikki, now ain't a good time, I got company. I'll call you later," my mama said blowing my Auntie off.

"On what? Yo damn phone has been off for months," Auntie Nikki called her out.

"Oh my god, Nikki, I'm busy, go head!"

"Janay, I'm not going no fucking where until we talk right fucking now!" my aunt raised her voice.

Suddenly I saw the door fly open and my mother stood there wearing a small tank top that hung loosely off her thin frame and a pair of shorts she had to hold up with her hands.

"What Nikki, damn? I'm busy," she complained.

"When's the last time you cooked? Or cleaned?" she asked.

"I don't fucking know? I'm doing the best I can," she lied.

"Look at X'Keem! Look, at his face, he looks so sad. Your lights are off, it stinks in here, it probably ain't no damn food..."

"What the fuck is your point?" she asked with an attitude.

"You need to step up and be a mother Janay. That boy over there needs you and what you doing ain't fair to him," Auntie Nikki said.

"If you would have just given me the fucking money for the abortion his ass wouldn't be here, now would he?" my mother asked her.

Aunt Nikki smacked the shit out my mama and my mama turned around to face her wolfing up like she was gone fight her. She might have been able to hurt my, underdeveloped ten-year-old body, but she was no match for my Auntie's thick adult frame.

"Mommy would be so ashamed of you!" Auntie Nikki told her as tears rolled down her face.

"Too bad mommy ain't here! If you think you can do a better job raising him then take his needy ass with you!" my mama screamed at her.

"Saint, pack yo stuff and say goodbye to yo raggedy mama," my Auntie told me.

My mama refused to meet my eyes when I looked at her to confirm that I was leaving.

"I need his Medicaid card, birth certificate, and social security card, too," my Auntie demanded.

She looked at me and nodded her head slowly.

"Pack everything you want to take with you and whatever you don't have I'll make sure you get it," she told me.

After that my mama really hit rock bottom. She chose to live on the streets instead of getting her shit together and being with me. Khalifa and Khadija and I were always close but living with them forged a different kind of bond. Even their daddy, Uncle David treated me like I was one of his own, so when they would go down to Atlanta to spend the summers with him, I was right beside them on the train. It didn't matter how close I was to them, it was still a part of me that didn't belong. And that part ate at me when I slept at night, when I saw family pictures and they all looked alike except me, and anytime I was alone.

Late one night after everybody had gone to bed, I was playing Russian Roulette with my Auntie's gun. I'd already shot four times and caught an empty chamber, so I had at least two tries left. The only problem was Auntie Nikki came home early. Just as I was squeezing the trigger, the gun went off, but just barely missed my head.

"What the fuck is wrong with you?" she yelled at me as she shook my shoulders. "What the fuck? Do you want to die?" she asked after she didn't get a response from me.

"DOES IT EVEN MATTER? WHO WOULD MISS ME IF I DID?" I screamed at her.

"Khalifa and Khadija for starters and yo uncle David for sure," she offered, trying to get me to smile.

"And if that ain't enough, then the next time you feel like that you let me be the reason you don't do it. Cause I'm crazy about you and I don't know what I'd do without you."

It would be my Auntie's words that would save my life over the years. I knew the desperation Sinna felt and I wanted to take that feeling away from her.

"Aight, I get it, we don't know each other like that. You got yo own drama to deal with, so you say, and I got some shit of my own too. I fuck with you though," I told her as I kissed her bare shoulder.

"What does that mean?" she asked with furrowed brows.

"It means when you get in yo feelings and you need a reminder, you can count on me," I told her.

"Look, I don't need another person in my life that's just going to let me down. I appreciate it, but I'll figure it out on my own," she said pulling away from me.

I pulled her body back to me, climbed between her legs, tangled my fingers in her dreads and stared deep in her eyes. Her fingers pushed my dreads back away from my face as I pushed inside of her slowly. Her eyes closed briefly before they fluttered back up and she nibbled on my bottom lip.

"Let me be the reason, baby," I moaned against her lips as I got lost inside her.

KHALIFA

KHALIFA

I don't know what the fuck Khadija was thinking about getting pregnant by that nigga Dirty, but she was gone have to dead that shit asap. I was against her fucking with him from the jump, but the bigger the deal I made out of her fucking with the nigga, the more she wanted to fuck with him. So, at my mama's request, I fell back and let her make her own mistakes, but this shit was going too fucking far.

I pulled up to the beat-up row house that had been passed down in his family and hopped out. I'd waited long enough to have this conversation, I hadn't pressed him about my sister because she claimed they were working shit out. Then today she comes in the house with a fucking bruise on her cheek, she claimed he ain't hit her, she got in a fight, but still, he had her out here fighting bitches just to keep his attention. That shit wasn't cool and even though I planned on cussing her ass out later, it was his turn now.

When I jumped out of my Land Rover and crossed the street, niggas popped up out of nowhere preventing me from walking up to the house.

"You lost ain't you homeboy?" Dirty asked from his position on the porch. I continued to walk towards him, bumping past the niggas he had clearly patrolling the street.

"Hold up," a tall dark skin guy said attempting to prevent me from getting to Dirty.

"You better get the fuck off of me before I beat the shit out of yo punk ass," I said pushing dude's hands off me.

"What's with all the hostility?" Dirty asked with a laugh, blowing out a cloud of smoke.

"You think I'm about to play with you? You put yo hands on my fucking sister?" I asked him as I pushed his bitch boy's hands off me for the second time. "I asked yo mans to keep his hands off me, I ain't asking again," I told him.

"Aye, my nigga I ain't holding a gun to nobody's head. I don't hit my women, Khadija jumped on my other baby mama, that's all. Don't worry, she won the fight," he laughed shaking his head.

"You better tread lightly fucking with my sister," I told him.

"Just like she made a choice to fuck me, she can decide not to, so take this petty shit up with her, not me," he said turning his back to me.

"Aight, you can play tough if you want, but I'll murder yo whole family without a second thought."

"Nigga, did you just threaten me? I thought we could co-exist, it's more than enough dope to go around; I planned to put you on," he smirked.

"Motherfucka, you barely got on yourself. And I don't make threats or promises, I predict the future," I told him stepping towards him again.

The black ass nigga that kept holding me back reached for me and pushed me back again. I pulled the Glock from my waistband, pointed at that nigga's head, and pulled the trigger dropping him instantly. Niggas rushed towards me ready to catch bullets before Dirty called them back.

"CHILL!" he yelled loudly.

"Nah, that nigga killed Black, you gone let that shit slide?" one of his niggas asked.

"DON'T FUCKING QUESTION ME!" Dirty yelled pulling a gun from his own waistband and dropping the nigga in front of him.

"Anybody else confused about what their position is?" he asked.

The niggas around me ain't even breath wrong in response.

"Pussy ass niggas," I laughed.

"I don't know if you heard or not, but I'm running shit round here now. This shit belongs to me," he told me.

"I don't give a fuck about your bullshit ass squad. I don't give a fuck about your mama or nobody else in your nothing ass family. If something happens to my sister, I'm not doing no talking. Take that shit how you like," I said before turning to walk back to my truck.

* * *

"That's right, eat my shit," I told Jasmine.

She was on her knees between my legs with my dick down her throat. Jasmine was a stalker, but she knew how to make me cum, so I usually had no objections to her being wherever I was.

"Damn." I groaned as my nuts started to tingle.

Two minutes later she held her mouth open while I fucked her face and she swallowed everything I gave her.

"You always taste sweet." She smiled lazily laying across my lap.

She leaned in to kiss my lips, but I stopped her.

"Fuck you doing, yo?" I asked with a concerned look on my face.

"Oh, you can't kiss me on the lips now?" she sassed propping a hand on her wide hips as she eyed me.

"Not after you been swallowing my babies." I mugged her.

"Khalifa!"

I'd been fucking with Jasmine for a minute, so she knew my rules, she knew what I liked, and she knew what I didn't, so why was she acting brand new? I swear females had a sixth sense called woman's intuition and it made them be able to tell when another woman was encroaching on her territory. I don't know if it was a scent they picked up, like dogs, but what I did know was that Jasmine's meltdown was all due to Money's infiltration on my life.

Yeah, I only fucked once, but in my dreams, I was fucking shorty every night. Outside of the fact she was built like a fucking stallion, Money was smart, she was just a hoe. Well, the daughter of a hoe anyway, and that was an issue for me because pimping was in my blood, part of the reason my daddy wasn't fucking with my mama back in the day was because she wasn't having that pimping shit. She forced him to make a choice and he chose making a life for himself. Sometimes his decision pissed me off other times it made me proud.

"Aye, I got some business to handle, I'll call you if I want you to come by, aight?" I asked now focusing my attention to where she stood beside me.

"You promise you gone call me?" she asked lowly.

As bad as Jasmine hated to admit it, I was daddy, she knew it and so did I.

"What did I say?" I asked while I stared into her eyes.

"See you later." She winked at me and walked out of my section in VIP.

Now, that she was gone I could focus on the task at hand, which was following a nigga that owed Ace money. I'd been following the nigga for a few days and his routine had been the same, work, home alone and then here to Sunshine. It was a hole in the wall strip joint that was a front for the hoes that was selling pussy. I knew I was pushing it being posted up here several nights in a row, but I had a job to do and that's what I was doing.

"What you doing here?" Rae asked as she hovered over the table, I was sitting in.

"Just working, Rae. I don't want no beef." I spoke up.

"You don't? I can't tell. You come here, to my shit and don't speak or nothing." She replied sitting down across from me.

Instantly, my attention diverted to the barely five-foot, shit-talking woman sitting across from me. I respected Rae, not like I had a choice cause she demanded respect above everything else. Rae was basically competition, her and my dad ran this area most of my life, the only reason I wasn't taking over for my dad was because my mama made me promise I'd be better than him.

My mama was the only thing keeping me back. Sure, I dibbled and dabbled here and there, but I help back mostly because I knew it would break her heart to see me out in the streets. A few months ago, she was diagnosed with a tumor on her spine, after a biopsy, we were told she had some kind of rare cancer that was in her organs and her blood. Of course, they offered Chemo and shit, that shit looked like it was killing her faster than the cancer was. If bills were late and needed to be paid, I could fix that, if the bathroom sink started running slow, I could fix that, but this Cancer shit was something I couldn't fix, it was nothing that I could do, except sit and wait.

"My fault, I should have spoke." I agreed as my eyes focused on my target that sat across the room.

"No maybe in that. How yo daddy doing?" she asked.

"He cool, I guess." I shrugged.

"I thought you were in here trying to recruit or something." She said eyeing me.

"Never that, Rae, give me some credit." I told her still watching my prey.

"You need some space?" she asked referring to the job at hand.

I shifted my eyes from the nigga pouring liquor on the women around him and focused on her briefly before I spoke.

"Nah, I ain't bringing no trouble yo way." I told her rising to my feet.

My target had run out of money to pay the women that were partying with him, so the woman began to drop off and disappear. Once he was alone, I decided to follow him out to the parking lot.

"Rae, Preciate it." I told her dropping a hundred on the table.

She simply nodded her head and watched me walk out the door. I could have included Saint and Kidd in tonight, but that would have made it three on one and for what? Just to say they were here? Nah, they was good wherever they were. After a few nights of watching his behavior, I was ready to move in on him, so I waited in his apartment for him to come home and catch the bullet I had for him.

"Demarcus, baby, I think you had too much to drink," a woman's voice called out.

"Girl, I'm good," he told her as they continued up the stairs and into the room, I was in.

"No, really, you're stumbling babe," she insisted.

Seconds later, I could hear their voices more clearly since they were in the same room as me. I couldn't see either one of them, but I could still hear their voices.

"Here sit down," she told him.

I heard the springs in the bed shift under his weight and I could hear him saying something to her.

"Why is the room spinning?" he asked.

"I told you, you had too much to drink babe," she repeated.

"Where you going?" he asked groggily.

"Nowhere baby," she said seductively.

While they went back and forth, I pulled the stocking cap down over my eyes and cocked my gun back just as I emerged from the closet.

"WHAT THE FUCK?" the nigga asked as he looked up at me with questioning eyes.

"You gotta pay what you owe," I shrugged.

"I don't owe nobody shit! You set me up didn't you bitch?" he fussed pointing at his girl.

I glanced at her and realized it was Money, the fine ass girl that was cool with some bomb ass pussy. She was fine as hell, but with a name like Money, I knew she was only about the cash and I was good on that shit. She had to be finessing this nigga, ain't no way she was serious about him.

"The fifteen you owe or your life," I told him plain and simple.

"I don't have it all, I got about eight in the safe," he mumbled.

"Fuck wrong with him yo?" I asked her watching him go in and out of consciousness.

"Nothing, he had a little too much to drink," she shrugged as she started going through his pockets.

He pushed away from her lightly, but he wasn't able to fight her off.

"Three hundred dollars! That's all you got?" she huffed hitting him in the stomach.

His eyes popped up for a second or two before he was back out of it.

"Is he dead?" I asked her.

"No, it's just a fucking muscle relaxant," she said rolling her eyes.

"You got the code to the safe?" I asked her as I walked over to the safe sitting in the closet.

"It ain't shit in there, but the deed to his funky ass house," she informed me. "The safe you're looking for is over there behind his self-portrait in the wall," she said pointing across the room.

I picked up a pillow and put it over his head before I fired two shots in that nigga's head, killing him instantly. I walked over to the picture and took it off the wall exposing the safe I would have never known was there.

"You got the—"

"Shut the fuck up! Gimmie the gun!" Money pushed her gun into the back of my head.

She snuck up on me from behind and now she had the upper hand.

"Money don't shoot me, baby," I told her as I rose from my squatted position.

"Nigga, I'ma splatter yo shit across this wall and leave yo ass stanking right beside that nigga over there," she told me as she took a step backward.

I turned around to face her and she snatched the panty-hose off my face.

"Khalifa?" she asked, surprised that it was me.

"I was surprised when I saw it was you finessing this nigga. That's how you get your money?" I asked putting pressure on her.

"Why are you here?" she asked still pointing the gun at me.

"Can you put the gun down, baby?" I asked her, stepping forward.

Now, the gun was pointed at the middle of my chest and touching my t-shirt.

"You came to kill me too?" she asked.

I gripped her wrist, pulling her towards me.

"I came here to get that nigga to pay what he owed, he ain't have it," I shrugged. "I ain't know you was here, but I'm glad you are. Without you, I wouldn't know shit about this safe. Open that bitch for me, baby," I told her.

"If I open it then we split whatever is in it," she said propping a hand on her massive hips.

I eyed her hips and ass before I nodded my head agreeing with her. She sashayed her pretty ass over to the safe and unlocked it for me. A few stacks of money sat inside it along with a money counter. I reached for it and Money stopped me putting her hand on mine.

"We gone count this shit right here," she told me.

I glanced behind her at the dead body lying on the bed.

"What you worried about that nigga for? He ain't going nowhere," she smacked her lips.

So, we counted the money right there on the floor, old school dollar for dollar.

"What yo pretty ass got going on?" I asked her as she rolled a blunt.

"Just trying to survive," she shrugged.

"This is a dangerous game you playing," I told her.

"I got this shit. I would have been in and out if you wouldn't have crept yo sneaky ass in here," she said with an eye-roll.

"Or that nigga could have overpowered you, raped you, beat yo ass and dropped you off in a landfill to die somewhere," I told her.

"Alright, *Crime Watch Daily*," she said rolling her eyes.

"This game ain't built on sympathy, these niggas don't give a fuck that you a woman. They'll bend yo ass over and take that shit before you process a thought, then what?" I asked her.

"Then I introduce them, niggas, to my baby," she smirked looking at the gun she had resting in her lap while she smoked.

"The shit you doing is dangerous, Money," I scolded her.

"I gotta get it how I live, my nigga. What you want me to do? Sit back and wait for some big dick nigga, with unlimited ends to fall out the sky and look out for a bitch?" she asked rolling her eyes.

"You ain't gotta be doing this shit, go to school, get a job—"

"I got a job, but thanks for the advice daddy," she said seductively winking at me.

"Yo, you always flirting and shit like you trying to get fucked, what's up?" I asked banding the last of the money together.

"Nigga, you been blowing me off all this time, go head," she blew me off as she blew out a smoke ring.

"I take it you was fucking this nigga, right?" I asked her, pointing at the dead nigga on the bed.

"Every now and then," she admitted.

"He fuck tonight?" I asked eyeing her juicy thighs that spilled out of the short two-piece skirt she wore.

She shook her head "no" slightly. I crawled over to her, not giving her time to move.

"Can I fuck you Money?" I asked.

My face was so close to hers our noses were touching. She nodded her head and parted her lips as she leaned back on her elbows and focused on me.

"I want my money first," she said dropping her eyes to the bag beside me.

I moved away from her and separated the six thousand dollars into three and slid her money to her. She thumbed it and then dropped it in her purse. I put the money in my pocket and rose to my feet before pulling her up to hers.

"Change yo mind?" she asked raising her eyebrows.

I wasted no time picking her up in my arms and burying my face in her neck, inhaling the fruity scent her skin was covered in. Her legs wrapped around my waist, pushing her skirt up around her waist exposing her bare ass. I could feel the heat from her pussy through my t-shirt. I snatched my shirt off and pinned her against the wall. She unbuckled my jeans and pulled my dick out as she stroked it.

"Damn, I miss that motherfucka." she moaned in my ear.

She positioned my dick outside her pussy teasing me.

"You sure you want to do this right here with him right here?" I asked.

Her eyes glanced at the body behind me briefly before she looked at me again.

"Ain't nothing wrong with an audience and like I said he ain't going nowhere," she shrugged.

Her response gave me the go-ahead so I pushed against her soft folds until I was as deep as I could go. Her body shuddered in my arms putting a smirk on my face that was hard for me to take off as I stroked her. The smacking sound of her pussy as my dick stirred that juicy motherfucka had me ready to split her ass I half. The room was quiet with only the sound of her pussy smacking as I dug into her.

"Shit." She hissed as her pussy started gripped my dick pulling us both into toe-curling orgasms.

* * *

"What up ma?" I asked when I walked into the house early that morning.

"You know what time it is Khalifa?" she asked as she moved round the small kitchen.

"How you feeling ma?" I asked ignoring her question.

"I'm fine, don't ignore my questions you know I hate that shit." She rolled her eyes.

"Ma, I know what time it is." I told her as I opened the refrigerator.

"Then you know better than to be creeping in my shit this late. You crawl out of some lil hoe bed to come home." She continued ranting.

"Ma, I love you." I told her kissing her jaw.

"I love you too. When I'm gone you better—"

"Ma! You ain't going nowhere. Chill, with that shit." I fussed.

"Your sister is pregnant. She ain't like you, she don't have that fight in her, she ain't ready to live on her own, Khalifa." She told me.

"I know ma, I got her, don't worry about her. I promise you I got her." I told her.

She shook her head no and then smiled at me.

"You can't force her to do something, you have to let her figure she needs help otherwise, she'll never see it." She told me.

"Yes, ma'am." I told her nodding my head accepting her advice.

7

____

KHADIJA

"Hello?" a female voice spoke into the phone.

"Who the fuck is this?" I spat with an attitude.

"Khadija, go to sleep honey, stop interrupting grown folks," Simone said into the phone.

"I need to talk to Dirty," I huffed.

"Well, you gone have to wait until the morning cause I put that nigga to sleep and he ain't waking up no time soon," she said and hung up the phone.

It was late, well after four in the morning, but I couldn't sleep. I knew Dirty was with her or at least I had a feeling anyway. He was splitting his time between the two of us and it was driving me crazy. I couldn't take it, I needed to know where Dirty was if he wasn't with me. He said I was thinking too much into it, he said he was just trying to keep the peace between us. I loved Sinna and it was out of respect for her that I didn't fuck her sister up sooner.

After getting dressed, I snuck out the house with Saint's

keys and drove his truck to Dirty's house to see if she was at his house or if he was at hers. Seeing his car parked outside his house pissed me the fuck off. How was he just keeping the peace having sleepovers with this bitch? I couldn't stop myself from calling back if I wanted to.

"Girl, it's too late to be up arguing about shit that ain't gone change," she laughed lightly.

"Bitch, when I see you I'ma fuck you up! You better ask Jessica about me hoe!" I told her.

"Girl, I ain't Jessica, come at me with that shit if you want to and I promise I'ma give you the ass whooping you deserve," she told me.

"Bitch, the sheets you in there laying on are covered in my pussy juice," I taunted her.

"Bitch, I smelled that fishy shit and told Dirty to throw them sheets in the trash. I ain't even want to wash that shit, you need to make an appointment at the clinic hun," she said.

"If I got something then both y'all gave it to me, cause Dirty the only nigga I been fucking," I spat.

"Whatever lil girl. I'm going to sleep now if that's alright with you," she said adding another laugh in before she hung up the phone.

I had so much shit to say to her, but I figured I was going to tell her face to face after Dirty left to handle his rounds in an hour or two. I sat in the truck crying over sad songs and hyping myself up until I watched his all-white old school Chevy pull out the driveway. Then I crept into the house through the unlocked door and stepped into the bedroom. I could hear Simone in the bathroom moving around.

"Talk all that shit you was talking now!" I yelled at her once she came out of the bathroom.

"BITCH!" she screamed grabbed the lamp beside her and throwing it at me.

It hit the side of me and bounced to the floor sending lightbulb and lamp pieces all over the floor.

I hit her with the lamp from the other side of the room and she charged me. I wasted no time punching her in the head and the side of her face, she attempted to hit me back, but she was mostly shielding her stomach. That's what I noticed, she was holding her round, very pregnant stomach. I pushed her away from me, getting ready to leave when she lifted her foot and kicked me in my stomach. I went reeling backward holding my stomach while she laughed.

"Get the fuck out of my house hoe!"

"This ain't yo shit bitch!" I screamed at her.

She waved her left hand at me showing me the ring on her finger.

"It will be soon enough, get lost bitch!" she growled at me as she rubbed her stomach.

I took a step towards her but stopped quickly when I felt like I was peeing on myself. My stomach cramped instantly, sending me into a hunched position as I held myself.

"You ain't strong enough for this shit, go get that rotten pussy checked hoe!" she said spitting in my direction.

My panties were soaking wet and not in a good way as I walked out of Dirty's house doing a duck waddle holding my stomach.

* * *

"You good?" my brother asked me as he met my eyes.

I shook my head no, refusing to speak. I'd been calling Dirty since the moment I drove away from his house. He refused to answer my phone calls, sending me to voicemail and shattering my heart each time.

"Damn, I'm sorry," Khalifa said dropping his head.

I touched his hand and nodded my head letting him know it was okay. Saint sat on the other side of me, and he grabbed my hand and kissed it softly too.

"You call Sinna and Money?" Saint asked.

"I texted them, but I told them I didn't want them to come up here right now. I don't want to talk, I just want to relax," I told them as I closed my eyes.

"Well, I sure hate it cause you gone at least hear my damn mouth!" Ma spat as she pushed her body off the wall and walked over to me.

"Ma, please—" Khalifa tried to get her to chill, but she cut that nigga off quickly.

"Shut the fuck up Khalifa, this my damn daughter and if I want to talk shit then that's what the fuck I'ma do!" she spat.

"Ma, don't you think I've been punished enough?" I asked her.

"No, I don't actually. You jump out here trying to be grown and shit but fall for the first dumb ass nigga that tells you he loves you. Dirty ain't even answering yo phone calls now. You out here having unprotected sex with a man who ain't worth a damn, he fucking everybody. That dick is for everybody!" she ranted while I tuned out most of what she was saying.

Not that I didn't know what she was saying was mostly true, because it was, but I was just sick of her saying it. I guess she figured the more she drilled her opinion of Dirty into my head the more I would listen to her, I don't know. I'd been in the hospital for more than seven hours and he still hadn't called, texted or come to make sure me or his child was okay. The longer I didn't hear from him the worse I felt.

"Khadija, you too smart for this kind of shit. Why would you be out here fighting with somebody when you know you're pregnant!" she hissed.

"And not just one fight, two fights," Saint added in.

"Don't you have somewhere to fucking be?" I asked him.

"Nope, I'm here with you," he told me.

"Oh, we all here with you cause we need to have a fucking talk with that nigga you claim to love so damn much!" my mother hissed.

"Ma, are you serious right now?" I asked her with wide eyes.

"You damn right I'm serious! You could have lost your life behind his bullshit! He out here dipping in you and then dipping here and there and you won't stand up for yourself, so I don't have a choice, but to cuss that nigga out for you!" she said.

I looked at Khalifa for help, but he turned his head and when I looked at Saint he just laughed and shook his head no. I pushed my body backward in the bed getting comfortable since she was going to be here all damn day.

A few hours later we were all taking naps when my phone started vibrating. I answered the phone and headed to the bathroom to have some privacy even though Khalifa and Saint claimed to be sleeping.

"Hello," I spoke lowly.

"What's up? Everything alright?" Dirty asked.

"No, everything is not fucking alright! I'm in the fucking hospital!" I barked.

"My baby alright?" he asked.

"I had a miscarriage," I told him lowly.

"That's yo own fucking fault!" he boomed at me. "I keep telling yo ass not to fucking stress about the shit that's going on, but you don't listen. Everything gotta be yo fucking way!" he scolded me.

"It ain't my fucking fault! Simone kicked me!" I spoke honestly.

"What? How she kick you?" he asked confused.

"I went to y'all house—" I told on myself as I started speaking.

"You went to my house? What the fuck is wrong with you?" he asked putting the blame back on me again.

"I called you cause I missed you and I wanted to tell you good night, she answered the phone. She was the one yelling about loving you and showing me the ring, you gave her and shit," I replied.

"I didn't want you to find that out like that," he replied.

"Then how would you have liked for me to find out? Send me an invite to the wedding or something?" I frowned.

"Khadija, I'm sorry, okay? I know it's no way I can make it up to you, but I'm really sorry, aight?" Dirty said sounding convincing.

"I hear you," I spat.

"You want me to bring you some candy and shit?" he asked.

"Khalifa and Saint are here right now, but I'll call you when they leave," I replied.

"Aight." He told me, and we hung up the phone.

SINNA

SINNA

I was trying to be there for Khadija while she was going through her miscarriage, but she was acting funny towards me and I was over the shit. I know the situation was kind of sticky since my sister and her shared a baby daddy, but she knew my situation with Simone. I hadn't seen her or Justyce in person since Christmas and it was a week before Valentine's day now. Sometimes when I called, she would answer, but most of the time she didn't. It wasn't about choosing aside for me, I was just trying to make sure I was supportive of my friend. I rode with Money to go check on Khadija even though she was texting Money, but not me. Getting to the hospital and seeing Saint's stupid ass sitting in the waiting room pissed me off.

I hadn't seen Saint since New Year's Day so, he was on my shit list now. He'd text me here and thereafter an IG post or after a few subliminal memes, but I didn't have a phone call or drop-in visit, nothing. I don't know why I was expecting more from him, but for some reason, I really was. I didn't know that much about him, so I didn't know why I was so stuck on him.

Now, seeing his stupid smile, broad shoulders, and dreads that clearly needed to be twisted had my pussy and my heart in overdrive. Even with his dreads being nappy and unkempt he was sexy as fuck.

"What room is she in?" Money asked aloud since Khalifa and Saint were just standing in the waiting room looking at us.

"Wassup Ma?" Saint asked rising to his feet and coming towards me.

"Nothing, what room is Khadija in?" I asked getting back to the point.

"I been meaning to call you," he was lying, but I was going to let him have it.

"You good; honestly I didn't expect you to call. We had sex; I mean it was good, but it was just sex," I shrugged.

He pulled me away from the group that was standing around focused on our conversation.

"Damn, just good? That's it?" he asked narrowing his eyes at me.

Earth-shattering, soul-stirring and had me dick drunk for days.

"What else were you expecting me to say?" I replied.

"The way you were hooping and hollering..." he started before I hit him playfully, cutting him off.

"Shut up!" I laughed, as I pushed him away.

"Can I see you tomorrow?" he asked me.

"Let's leave sex as just sex. No need to fuck up a good thing." I replied trying to step away.

I moved away from him, but Saint held my hands as he focused on me.

"Is sex all you want?" he asked.

"Clearly that's all you're giving," I replied.

"Touché," he agreed, raising both hands in the air. "You should let me come see you tonight."

"Are you asking me out on a date or..." I started to ask with a blank face.

"Honestly, I want to talk. I got a phone full of females I

can have sex with. You seem like you're a good listener," he spoke quietly.

"Aight," I agreed rolling my eyes.

I should have cussed his pretty ass out and told him to kick rocks, but I didn't I nodded and grinned like the dick drunk bitch he'd made me.

* * *

I tried to be there for Khadija, but she was short and choppy with me, barely looking me in the face, and talking to me like she didn't really know me like that. I decided to give her a couple of days to get her mind together before I called her out on her shit, plus I needed to get myself together and catch up on some homework if I was going to be spending the night with Saint. So, I did my homework, washed my sheets, and cleaned the house top to bottom while I waited for him to call me or come by. I finally decided to go to sleep after seeing him partying with his boys in the club all night. The next day I was standing in the mirror styling my hair with AJ on speakerphone begging to spend time with me.

He was still hanging around, I was leading him on while Saint was doing the same with me. It was sad really, but AJ was a good distraction and he liked to spend money on me so, I was cool with fucking with him.

"I really need you tonight," Money said coming to me while I lay across my bed.

"Need me to do what?" I asked raising an eyebrow.

"You on the phone?" she asked.

"Yeah."

"Ah, shit I'll call you later, Sinna." AJ spoke up hearing Money in my background.

I laughed at his response, "bye." I told him before I hung up.

"I just need you to go on a date for me, I have another

date scheduled, but I can't reschedule because he ain't from round here," she told me.

"You are really pushing it," I told her as I left out the bathroom and sat down on the bed. "What do you want me to do?" I frowned.

"He'll be at the bar wearing a black suit and—"

"Money, you gone owe me if I do this shit for you!" I barked, sitting up off the bed.

"It's more like a sympathy date and I'll be in the same restaurant, just with another date." she smiled, jumping on me and hugging my neck.

"Yeah, whatever. The second I feel uncomfortable, I'm leaving," I warned her.

"I think you'll be just fine," she smiled brightly at me.

"Whatever," I rolled my eyes at her.

Later that night I was standing in the bathroom doing my makeup when a message from Saint came through.

Saint: I miss the taste of my pussy.

"Damn, I love the way you feel," Saint growled in my ear from behind me as he pounded my pussy.

My back arched, and my nipples were so hard they ached as I remembered how good his body smelled as he did push-ups on top of me. My body shuddered at the memory of him being deep inside of me.

Me: I got a date tonight, but I'll text you when I get back home, cool?

Saint: No, the fuck it ain't cool, my nigga.

Me: I don't stop you from living yo life. You just wanna fuck! Let me try to find a nigga that wanna talk to me.

Me: And stop calling me! I'm trying to do my make up!

Saint: You always look good, it ain't nothing you can do to enhance what God already gave you, girl.

Me: Corny ass!

Me: Thanks…I'll text you later.

Saint: Where you going with ole boy?

Me: I'm not telling you shit.

Saint: Aight, bet.

He didn't text anything else, that didn't stop me from constantly checking my phone to see if he'd texted. Finally, after making sure my makeup was on point, I opened the front door prepared to leave until I came face to face with Saint.

"Wassup baby?" he asked with a smile as he opened his arms wide in an attempt to hug me.

"What are you doing here?" I asked pushing him away from me.

"Where yo pretty ass going?" he asked with a smirk on his face.

"Nigga, what are you doing here?" I repeated adding a frown.

It was hard to form a frown seeing him standing in front of me blinding me with his pretty ass jewelry, hid dreads retwisted and pulled up into a style, and his body dipped in the cologne that kept Ms. Kitty going crazy.

"Damn it's like that?" he asked matching my frown.

"Hell yeah, it's like that. Look, I got somewhere to be, I can't do this with you right now," I replied tucking my clutch under my arm and pulling my door closed.

I inhaled the scent of his cologne that use to coat my sheets. I missed it, but I couldn't give into Saint and his hoe shit.

"Stop!" I laughed as he wrapped his arms around me and picked me up spinning me around.

"Fuck that," he said putting me down and turning me to face him.

Before I could push him away, he had his tongue down my throat.

"Damn, I missed kissing you," he said against my lips.

"Stop, don't say shit you don't mean," I blurted out.

"What makes you think I didn't miss kissing you?" he asked looking at me with those hypnotizing eyes of his.

"Don't worry about it," I told him attempting to walk past him.

"Nah, answer me," he said standing in the way.

"I'm already late, I gotta go," I told him shifting my weight from one foot to the other.

"Not until you answer me. Now what's up?" he asked positioning his legs in a wide stance.

"I don't want to get attached or start catching feelings for you when this thing between us is just going to be sex." I told him.

"What you want from me yo? I thought we was cool," Saint replied.

"I don't just let niggas fuck me, especially not raw. And I let you and then you disappear on me. You were all, *let me be the reason*, a month ago and now you gone," I shrugged.

"I ain't trying run game on you ma or nothing like that. Real g-shit, I feel different when I'm with you. I ain't never felt like I could be myself with a female like I feel when I'm with you," he told me.

"And that shit sounds good and all, but I'm not about to be sitting around waiting on you. I'm not saying I'm ready to jump in a relationship, but I ain't about to put my life on hold for you either," I shrugged.

"If that's what you waiting on then you gone be waiting forever. I told you before I'm just chilling right now. I got a lot of shit on my plate and I can't be trying to make that kind of move. I can't put you in a harm's way like that," he replied.

"I don't understand. I'm not trying to jump into a relationship with you tomorrow, but I mean eventually, that's the goal, right?" I asked.

"Why what we doing need a title? If you looking for a man to give you a title then I ain't him, ma. The label doesn't mean shit if the nigga behind it ain't solid." he told me.

"I get it, but I want the relationship that goes with the title I ain't tryna be nobody's fuck buddy forever." I stated.

"And my hand to god I want you to be so much more. But right now, ain't the time to give up or get soft, I gotta keep everything around me untouchable. You important to me, why you can't just leave it at that?" he asked before placing a juicy kiss on my lips. "Now, you gone let me in, so I can make love to you or we gone stand out here talking all night?" he asked.

"I told you I got a date," I laughed.

"With who? That nigga AJ?" he asked. "You ain't think I knew that shit?" he asked.

"It doesn't matter, you ain't trying to be my nigga, right?" I asked with a shrug as I tried to walk past him.

"You just gone walk past me?" he asked following me as we walked down the stairs.

"I'll call you later," I offered once we reached the bottom.

"Gimme a kiss before you go," he demanded, pulling me back to him.

"One kiss," I told him as he closed the space between us.

He kissed me once and then twice before he gripped my ass cheeks and pushed our foreheads together.

"Call me when you get back," he told me before he walked away.

* * *

An hour later, I was sitting at a table in *Salt and Lime Cabo Grill* wishing I could blow my fucking brains out. The nigga I was sitting across from was so self-centered he'd been talking since I sat down. I was late due to Saint's silly ass, but I felt like I jumped in on an already going conversation. The shit was crazy.

"Yeah, I been living in Raleigh since I was twelve, but I've been living in Durham for a few years now. Where did you say you lived again?" he asked leaning forward as if I told his weird-ass where I lived to begin with.

"I didn't," I replied sipping the ginger ale I was drinking.

"Either way, if you plan on moving to an area that's really on the rise then I can put you in touch with a great realtor. She's a little long-winded, but she's amazing and she knows what she's talking about too," he replied with a smile. "Is this your first-time online dating?" he asked.

"No—Yeah," I nodded.

"Really? What made you want to do online dating? I mean you're so pretty, I'm sure you don't have trouble with men," he said giving me a creepy smile with his thin, crusty lips pressed together.

He was leaning so far over, the balding section of his head was exposed, his nicotine and coffee-stained teeth formed a sneer, and his pointed nose was pushed higher than it usually was, giving me a view of the small booger that was tangled in his nose hair.

"Aye, what the fuck is this?" Saint's voice boomed throughout the restaurant.

My head snapped backward in his direction as he stomped towards me with a deep scowl on his face.

"What the fuck you doing having dinner with my fucking wife?" he barked at my date.

At this point, I couldn't even remember the nigga's name, but even if I could it wouldn't matter cause I was beyond ready to go home. Money was just about to get a bad rating from this nigga cause I couldn't take this shit any longer.

"I'm sorry for this," I told the guy across from me.

"Sorry? You gone apologize to this motherfucka?" Saint asked stepping towards the guy.

The guy backed away with a terrified look on his face while Saint was smiling.

"I'm ready—"

"Is this the nigga that gave you the STD you gave me? You tell this creepy motherfucka to get checked?" Saint asked looking from me and then back at the man.

"Okay, jokes over, you doing way too much now," I told Saint.

I looked at my date and he glanced at me with sympathetic eyes.

"I don't have an STD," I gritted.

"It's okay if you—"

He stopped speaking when Saint moved in front of him and grilled him.

"I mean, it's not okay. I—I—"

"You what, nigga? You got an issue with my girl?" Saint asked him almost hovering over the man.

"Stop it, jackass!" I spat, pushing Saint away from the man who looked like he was about to piss himself any minute.

"You really thought I was gon let you go on a date with another nigga? I wish it had been that nigga AJ you was here with." Saint spat grilling me.

"You got some issues for real," I said as I turned around and picked up my wine glass off the table and tossed back what was left of my ginger ale.

Just as I was heading out of the restaurant, I was lifted off my feet by Saint and put over his shoulder where he smacked my ass repeatedly as he led me out the restaurant with everyone's eyes on us.

Once we were outside in the parking lot, he put me down and busted out laughing.

"It's not funny psycho! That man was really on a date looking for love and you just embarrassed him for a laugh." I shook my head as I power walked away from him.

"I don't give a fuck if you were on a date with a cancer patient or not, you gone learn if I want something, I get it," he said with a wild look in his eye.

"You make me sick!" I yelled at him.

"I'ma make you love me, girl," he told me.

"I doubt it." I tossed back rolling my eyes.

"That defiant shit you keep doing, gone make us parents, stop playing with me." He demanded putting me back over his shoulder and walking over to his truck.

8

————————

MONEY

"*D*amn, y'all pretty," some nigga with blond tips on the ends of his curly fade complimented us.

Khadija, Sinna and I were walking through Crabtree Valley mall when this nigga and his little friends decided to harass us. Sinna and Khadija tried to be polite to them, but I wasn't feeling it. I was on a mission to find the perfect dress to hide a few weapons in, but I wasn't having much luck. I could always wear something I had in my closet, but I was trying to be more careful with the way I was moving, since I'd robbed a good handful of niggas now.

Yeah, I hard Khalifa loud and fucking clear when he said the shit, I was doing was dangerous, but I couldn't help myself. My girls didn't want to get in on the credit card scamming idea I had, so this was the next best thing. I'd set up a few different profiles on some sugar baby websites hoping to catfish some niggas and so far, I was doing good.

"I'm walking in Zale's next, who's buying?" I asked

looking from one face to another of the little niggas standing in front of me probably living with their baby mamas.

"Hold up, I just met you ma," the nigga in the middle replied raising his hands.

"It was nice meeting you, but we have things to do," I hissed pulling Khadija and Sinna past Zale's, continuing our hunt for the dress I was looking for.

"Damn, Money, that's fucked up," Sinna laughed.

"Girl, you ain't thinking about that nigga no way, you too sprung on Saint's crazy ass," I called her out.

I heard them fucking damn near every night, just like I'm sure she heard me and Khalifa the few times he'd actually spent the night. I'd fucked with my share of hustlers before, but Khalifa was a different breed which was part of my attraction to him. He was straightforward, but he knew how to sit back and watch shit too. I loved how thuggish he was even when he wasn't trying to be hard. He was funny, but unintentionally which only made him funnier.

"Like you ain't hitting Ariana Grande notes when Khalifa locked in the room with you, bitch," she tossed back.

"Eww," Khadija said scrunching her nose as she shook her head.

While we went store to store looking for the perfect dress for me, I saw Saint and Khalifa walk past the store with two females in stride with me.

"Bitch come one," I said grabbing Khadija's and Sinna's hands and leading them out of the store.

"What—" Sinna started to ask before her eyes landed on Saint.

He was holding the girl to his right by her wide hips with a smile on his face.

"This nigga can't be serious," she said tilting her head.

Khalifa was sitting down eating a pretzel while the girl he was walking with stood in between his gapped bowed legs eating an ice cream cone.

"Oh, nah, them niggas serious," I said taking my earrings off.

I knew I probably didn't have a right to be upset, but I couldn't help but be in my feelings seeing the nigga that was sucking my soul through my pussy at night using them same lips to talk to another bitch. Yeah, that shit was blowing the fuck out of me.

"Y'all, all these street dudes are just alike. They use you, lie to you and ain't none of it worth nothing, my brother and cousin included," Khadija said.

"I still say you should have fucked Dirty up, shit you should have let dirty dick Khalifa do it," I said rolling my eyes as I watched Khalifa smack the girl's ass.

"Y'all ready?" Sinna asked once she'd pulled her dreads back.

"Yup," I nodded.

We walked over to the boys, I wanted to bust out laughing seeing the look on Saint's face when he saw Sinna standing in front of him. Khalifa looked cool as a cucumber which pissed me off. He took another bite of his pretzel as his eyes roamed my body from the seat where he was planted.

"What y'all buying from here?" Sinna asked pulling at the bag in Saint's hands.

"Not shit really," he replied letting her roam through his bag.

Khalifa and I stood locked in a stare-off battle I refused to lose.

"What you buying?" he asked licking his lips.

"Some work clothes," I replied with a grin.

"What you doing?" Khalifa asked as he lay beside me.

"Setting my alarm clock, I got an early day," I told him putting my phone on the nightstand beside him.

"I thought you only worked second shift at Wendy's?" he asked me.

"Don't be clocking my damn schedule," I said with a laugh. "I do a little more than just work at Wendy's."

"I figured that much," he replied.

"What do you do?" I asked putting the heat on him.

"I do it all baby," he told me, teasing a nipple before inhaling it into his mouth.

"Shit," I hissed, arching my back off the bed. "That's not answering my question though," I finally said once he pulled away.

"What you want from me?" he asked.

"It's a pretty simple question, I mean you don't have a job—"

"I do whatever I gotta do to get what I need. I'm a hustler, baby I can sell water to a whale," he said laughing.

"Me too, my mama started calling me Money cause she said no matter where we were or what we were doing I found a way to make a dollar or two," I laughed.

"Damn, you always been getting to the money, huh?" he laughed with me, tossing his dreads back.

"Hell yeah."

"Now, you out here finessing these niggas, separating them from that paper? I ain't knocking it, shit you gotta get it how you live," he shrugged.

"I wasn't gone kill Demarcus," I offered.

I actually did feel bad that he was dead, he was cool, and he actually didn't mind spending money on me. I'd been pulling a few hundred out his pockets while he slept and out the safe when I spent the night at his house. Khalifa killing him actually put me in a bind, but I was grateful he was a man of his word and split it with me.

"Shit, you a fool for not killing the nigga. He knew yo name—"

"I wasn't going to empty his safe or nothing," I shrugged.

"If you gone be out here robbing these niggas then you gotta be smart, you gotta protect yo self—"

"You think I don't know how to protect myself?" I asked climbing into his lap and straddling him.

"I hope you do, shit you still need backup. You out here doing this shit by yourself," he said moving my hair from my face with one hand.

"You might be right about that," I replied biting my bottom lip.

"But don't be bringing my baby sister in that shit, she ain't ready for no shit like that," he told me.

"Okay," I replied with a head nod.

"I'm serious Money," he said resting his hand on my face.

"I said okay, Khalifa," I replied rolling my eyes.

"Hey, I'm Khadija. I'm Khalifa's sister and Saint's cousin, what's your name?" Khadija broke the silence introducing himself to the bitches in front of us.

"I'm Trina and that's my bestie Nina," Khalifa's girl said with a smile.

"Khadija, what's up y'all good?" Saint asked.

All the conversations were going on around us while I stared directly at Khalifa and he stared back at me, neither one of us saying anything.

"Yeah, we straight. What y'all about to do?" Khadija asked.

"Well, I been promising Khalifa a taste of my famous fried chicken, so I was gone, cook—"

"Fried chicken? Bitch ain't nothing special about fried chicken. You season the shit, coat the shit, and drop it in grease, it ain't rocket science," I spat finally directing my attention to the girl still standing between Khalifa's legs.

"I mean maybe when you cook it, but—"

I didn't wait for her to finish her sentence before I slapped the ice cream cone out her hand, knocking it to the floor after bouncing off Khalifa's leg.

"Are you serious?" she asked with a shocked expression on her face.

Khalifa stood as if him standing would change anything I was going to say or what I was going to do.

"Money—"

I cut his sentence off by picking up the ice cream cone and sending it crashing into his little girlfriend's face. It hit her with a loud smack before it rolled down her clothes putting a smile on my face.

"What the fuck is wrong with you?" Khalifa asked gripping my wrists tightly.

"Ain't shit wrong with me, I'm good," I smirked.

"Who the fuck is this bitch anyway?" the girl asked appearing over his shoulder.

"I'm that sweet smell on his lips, that same smell that's entangled in all that thick dick hair, I'm the scratches and the hickeys on his body, bitch remember my face cause every time you see this nigga, you better remember that's all me," I told her before snatching my wrist from him and storming off.

* * *

"You ever wish you ain't know some shit about a nigga, cause you want shit to go back to the way it was?" Khadija asked later than night.

"Hell no, fuck that! I want to know everything," I said shaking my head.

"So, you cool with Khalifa fucking with the baddest bitch?" Khadija asked referring to the bitch that was with Khalifa named Trina.

"Long as he wrapping my dick up when he fucking them hoes that ain't half of me, I'm cool," I shrugged.

I was lying. That shit was eating me up slowly, but what was I supposed to say? He made it very clear from the first time we fucked that he was only interested in fucking and to a certain extent, I felt the same way. But seeing him standing next to a bitch I knew he was fucking sent a rage through me that I almost couldn't control.

"Sinna, you mighty quiet," I noticed watching her texting on her phone.

"Cause her and Saint over there texting each other back and forth," Khadija said rolling her eyes.

"You know what your problem is?" Sinna asked looking at Khadija.

"What?" Khadija asked.

"You let Dirty do shit and you never got any get back. I

146

get it, you love him, you lost a baby, and he broke your heart, but that nigga ain't shit and he ain't gone be no better for the next bitch," Sinna shrugged.

"She right," I agreed.

"So, what am I supposed to do? Go out here and fuck another nigga?" she asked rolling her eyes.

"I mean if you want to, but I say we go fuck up his car. Niggas love their cars," Sinna said with a smile. "Plus, if I don't get out some of this energy Ima fuck around and fuck Saint ass up."

"I don't think that's a good idea," Khadija laughed.

"Fuck that nigga! He doesn't take care of my nephew and he got you and my sister hating each other cause he can't keep his dick out of either one of y'all. If you ain't gone fuck up his car then I will," Sinna said hopping up from her seat.

"What?" Khadija asked confused.

"Shit, I'm with Sinna, let's go," I agreed.

We left out and headed over to the apartment Dirty shared with Sinna's sister and parked beside Dirty's Charger.

"Now what?" Khadija asked.

"Gimme that damn milkshake," Sinna said reaching for the large Oreo blast we got from Sonic.

She got out of the car and drizzled the ice cream from the front of the car all the way to the back. I got out the car with the Snickers in my hand, opened it, took a bite and then popped the gas door to drop it inside. Khadija got out of the car with a bottle of water and a screwdriver in her hand. She poured the water into the gas tank and went to the back of the car and took off the license plate.

"We should have got some damn bologna," I said shaking my head once we were back in the car.

"True, but I think we did a good job—"

"Nah, hold up," Khadija said jumped out the car.

She stabbed all the tires with the screwdriver just as a car came speeding into the parking lot. She jumped in the car and we drove off with the car right behind us. I tried turning quickly, but the car was following us as we whipped through traffic.

"Oh, shit! You think it's him?" Khadija asked as she looked out the back window.

"Who else could it be?" Sinna asked shaking her head.

"Well, that nigga need to fall back, straight up," I said running a red light with his ass on my tail.

"Turn right here," Sinna told me pointing to the entrance of an alley.

I followed her instructions and the car behind us continued going straight unable to turn quick enough or back up since it was a one-way street. We continued down the alley laughing until we continued on our trip back to my house.

"WHERE THE FUCK YOU BEEN?" Khalifa yelled the second I walked into my house.

"What that fuck? How you get in here?" I asked as we all walked in.

"Mama okay?" Khadija asked with wide eyes.

"Yeah, she good, here take my truck and go home." He told her handing her his keys.

"Damn, I gotta go y'all." Khadija said with a laugh.

Seconds later I heard Saint's deep voice talking to Sinna as she walked into her bedroom.

"Y'all niggas really just broke in my shit, like that's cool?" I asked him.

"I asked you a question yo," he said clenching his jaw.

"How you get in my house?" I asked him as I walked towards him.

"I ain't gone repeat myself," he replied lowly.

I ignored him and walked past him into the kitchen to put the tray of milkshakes we got from Cook Out in the freezer. When I turned around Khalifa was standing behind me.

"You had my sister out doing hoe shit?" he quizzed pushing our noses together.

"What?" I asked pushing him out my face.

"You fucking heard me!" he growled.

"Khalifa, what are you talking about?" Khadija asked him with a frown.

"Where were you?" he repeated still looking at me.

"In my skin," I told him, refusing to give him a play by play of my whereabouts.

Khadija pulled on his arm trying to get his attention and get him to back away, either way, I wasn't backing down. Khalifa's problem was he wanted me to be calling him and acting a fool like I cut up earlier in the mall. I wasn't going to do that shit though, I made my point in the mall. He could fuck that girl all he wanted because at the end of the day he was going to end up right here in my face, trying to get in my bed one way or another.

"Let me go," he told Khadija as he snatched away from her.

"Aww, you mad?" I laughed before I blew him a kiss.

"Oh, it's funny? I'm mad you out here showing my sister—"

"Nigga, she ain't five! Khadija is a grown-ass woman, she can do whatever the fuck she wants, where yo bitch at? That's who you need to be monitoring." I said staring into his eyes.

"She at home recovering from the dick down I gave her," he smirked.

I laughed instead of smacking him like I wanted to do.

"Her special chicken was probably cat from the Chinese food place," I said rolling my eyes.

"At least she knows how to be a woman. I ain't got to worry about her fucking for cash," he replied.

"Aye, hoe is life," I said bending over and twerking.

His words actually hurt my feelings, but I'd never show him that. Fuck him and fuck her too. If he wanted her, then fuck him. Ain't no way he was going to just hurt my feelings and then move on with his little ghetto barbie doll. If he wasn't fucking me then he wasn't going to fuck anybody happily.

"Let's go Khadija before I have to kill this girl," he said brushing past me.

"Fuck you, Khalifa! And for the record, I don't fuck for money, but you know what? Maybe I should shit the way my box had you moaning," I said with a laugh.

"Niggas don't wife hoes, we fuck 'em," he said stepping back in my face.

"I ain't worried, you won't be fuckin' that one for long," I shrugged.

"Fuck that mean? That supposed to be a threat or something?" he asked humored by my words.

"Good night Khalifa," I grinned at him.

I pushed past him and opened the front door for him to step out of it. He walked to the door and stopped as he looked at me with questioning eyes.

"Don't bother that girl, Money. You got an issue with me, take that shit up with me," he said protecting his little bitch.

"That's how you feel? I might actually have to kill this bitch," I said more to myself than to him.

"Girl, go head, you ain't about to kill nobody," he said shaking his head.

"Guess we just have to wait and see," I said matching the slick grin on his face.

KHADIJA

KHADIJA

"You gotta stop hanging with Money and Sinna," Khalifa tried to tell me the next day.

"Boy, you need to go head and have some kids since you think you can tell me what to do," I blew him off as I pulled my drink out the refrigerator.

"Khadija, Money into some shit you ain't ready for," he replied.

"Where Kidd?" I asked him, changing the subject.

"Why? You feeling him?" Khalifa asked.

"And if I am?" I asked propping my hand on my hips.

"Why you keep trying to fuck with these street niggas? You ain't learned we ain't shit?" he asked looking at me.

"You shouldn't have said the shit you said about Money. You know she don't be fucking for money," I scolded him.

"Shit, she might as well be fucking for it," he shrugged.

"She ain't perfect, but she got a good heart and she cares about you," I told him.

"That's like the first rule of hustling yo," he said shaking his head.

"What?" I asked.

"You can't wife a hoe," he said like that shit was written in stone or something.

"First of all, Money ain't a hoe. You ever heard about her? I mean seriously, have you?" I asked him.

"Just cause niggas ain't talking shit about fucking her, don't mean she ain't out here fucking." he shrugged.

"Remember to tell yourself that when she's off loving somebody else," I told him before I walked out the room.

* * *

"Where you been?" I asked Kidd as he lay across my bed later.

"Fuck you mean?" he asked looking at me with a frown.

"I mean normally you be stuck up Khalifa's ass. You and Saint both been missing lately, but you more so than anybody," I explained.

"We got some new shit we working on, that's all," he shrugged.

"New shit? What you mean?" I asked sitting up on the bed.

Kidd was leaning on his forearm watching me while I spoke. The most we'd ever done was kiss and almost fuck, but only because he stopped us from going further. Everything about Kidd as sexy as hell, down to his thick, curly eyelashes that he batted at me constantly. He was the best friend I could talk to and tell everything to, but the nigga I wanted to fuck at the same time.

"You nosy as fuck," he laughed.

"I'm just trying to figure out what's going on with you. I mean one minute I feel like everything is cool with us and then the next I can't find you for shit," I pointed out.

"I admit I have been busy, but I'm always thinking about you," he said touching my face with his hand.

"You say that, but you don't call or nothing. A bitch don't get a smoke signal or nothing," I said shaking my head.

"Aight, you right. I know I been slack, but straight up, I fell back cause I ain't trying to bring you in my shit." he explained staring into my eyes.

"I don't know what that even means," I said shaking my head and getting off the bed.

"You don't know what's best for you? I thought you wanted to be a fashion designer? Ain't that why you always drawing and window shopping for shit you know you can't afford? Or a hairdresser shit you always doing hair. Focus on that shit, don't worry about me." Kidd asked putting a smile on my face.

"You get on my damn nerves," I said rolling my eyes.

"You love a nigga though and you know I'm right." he said moving to stand beside me near the window.

"You give yourself way too much credit," I told him.

"So, you don't love a nigga?" he asked wrapping his arms around me and pulling me against him.

He stared at me while he waited for the response, he already knew the answer to. He knew I loved him, hell anybody with eyes could tell I loved him. And I knew he loved me too.

"I don't know why I love you," I said pushing away from him.

"Oh, you don't?" he asked with a smile as he pulled me back in.

"No. You barely kiss me, you won't fuck me, and you damn sure won't be with me," I said staring into his eyes.

He looked away from me and exhaled a deep breath.

"You don't know how bad I want you. I wish it was simple as just kissing you, just fucking you, but it ain't. I want you all the fucking time," he told me licking his lips.

"So, be with me, fuck me, love me," I demanded standing in his face.

"I don't deserve you. I ain't shit and I ain't gone be shit. You deserve a man that's gone love you the way you need to be loved. I'm not that man," he said, shaking his head.

"Why not? What's wrong with me? Why you can't love me?" I asked.

My heart was breaking the more he explained how he felt. Why couldn't he just be whatever he felt like I needed since I deserved so much? He was talking in riddles and the shit was pissing me off.

"Ain't shit wrong with you. Don't you ever let anybody tell you any different, you're perfect. Every pimple, every black-head, mole, scratch, scrape, all of it. I love every part of you from the inside out," he said kissing me softly.

His mouth tasted like weed Hennessey and I loved it. I wanted the kiss to last forever. He kept pulling away, but I wouldn't let him pull away from me, I followed him until we were back laying across my bed with me straddling his lap in only a pair of pajama pants and a bra.

"Why you making this shit so hard?" he asked finally ending the kiss and kissing my forehead.

"Making this hard? Please, that's you making it hard." I laughed referring to his hard dick that was poking my pussy.

I positioned my body directly over it so that he and I both would be able to feel his dick pushing against my pussy. I started a slow grind that he encouraged by gripping my hips and biting his bottom lip.

"Fuck me," I moaned as I sat up.

"Khadija—"

I cut off whatever he was going to say by unhooking my bra and taking it off.

"Damn, you got some pretty ass titties," he told me massaging them with his big hands.

"Trey, baby I need you so bad right now," I groaned pressing my bare chest against him as I kissed his lips.

"I need you too baby," he told me helping me out of my pajama pants.

His voice was hoarse, low, but firm, setting my body on fire.

He took his jeans off and pushed them down his muscular, brown thighs and kicked them off the bed. I gripped the long-extended pipe below me and stroked it while I stared into his eyes.

"Sit on my face," he demanded.

I started my climb up his long body before he stopped me and forced me to turn around. I kissed down his muscular chest before my lips found his dick. I couldn't keep my eyes open as he spread my pussy and lapped at my juices.

"Fuck," he groaned as I worked him in my mouth.

My mouth gripped him as my hands stroked his thickness. Once I was finally comfortable with his size, I deep throated him.

"Baby, slow down or I'ma nut," he panted.

My pussy throbbed and ached as he tongue fucked me and used his thumb to massage my clit. Seconds later I was cummin' and barely stroking his dick.

"I can't believe I been missing out on that," he groaned in my ear once I'd crawled to the end of the bed.

He gently turned me over to my back and spread my legs, kissing my ankles, then my calves, and finally my thighs. He kissed my pussy softly sending shock waves through me as he used his mouth to make love to my pussy. Finally, after I came a second time, he moved up my body to my stomach that was still heaving from the pleasure he'd given me up to my hardened nipples and finally stopping to kiss my lips as he rested between my thighs.

"Fuck me," I moaned against his lips.

He slid just the tip of his dick inside me slowly before sliding the rest of him inside me in one quick push.

"Fuck," I moaned loudly.

"Shush," he whispered as he covered my mouth with his, effectively silencing my moans.

His strokes were deep and hard, especially since I was meeting him halfway. He stared down in my eyes as our bodies rocked against each other thrust for thrust and moan for moan. He flipped me over on my stomach and pulled my knees up. He pushed deep inside of me no longer moving slowly and instead of pounding me from behind like he was going to nut in seconds but stopped suddenly and pulled out and kissed my ass cheeks one at a time. He spread my legs wider and slid underneath me. He wrapped his entire mouth around my pussy, making my eyes roll as he tried to suck me dry.

"How it taste?" I moaned.

He stuck two fingers inside me, pulled them out, and pushed his fingers towards me. I inhaled the scent my juices emitted from his fingers before I lowered my head and licked his fingers clean. He slid back on his elbows and pulled himself up before he sat up with his back flat against the headboard.

"Get on top baby," he demanded.

His eyes were closed, his bottom lip tucked as he held my waist tight while I bounced up and down on his dick.

"God damn," he said smacking my ass when I turned around on his dick with no hands.

I held his claves for balance while he smacked my ass and gripped it in his hands helping to balance me.

"You love me baby?" he asked smacking my ass once more.

I nodded my head as I felt another orgasm rumble through my body.

"Tell me," he demanded.

"I love you, Trey," I called out as I came.

"Fuck, I love you too," he squeezed out before he was cummin' with me.

After that, we were both passed out beside each other in the bed. I don't know who fell asleep first, but we were both knocked out at some point. I woke up a couple of hours later to get a bottle of water. When I came back to my bedroom, I saw his phone lighting up inside his jeans. I wanted to ignore it, everything inside of me was screaming that I needed to ignore it, but my feet took me over to his jeans anyway. I started to walk away, but it lit up again, so I pulled the phone out of his jeans and looked at the display. The phone said he had several missed calls all from the same unprogrammed phone number. I wanted to call the number back and see who it was. My eyes darted over to him to make sure he was asleep, I watched Kidd's chest rise and fall while he snored.

I lay back down in the bed beside Kidd and rested my head on his shoulder while I watched him breathe. I used a finger to trace a trail from his beard down to the middle of his chest. I planted kisses down the trail and then closed my eyes as I prepared myself to fall asleep. Just as I started to doze off, it came to me whose phone number that was.

"SIMONE!" I gasped sitting up in the darkness.

9

———

KHALIFA

"**D**amn, I can't breathe you so deep baby," she groaned as I stroked her.

I heard what Money said and a part of me felt bad for hurting her feelings, but she needed to understand that I wasn't one of them niggas she met online and bitched out of some money. I was a real nigga and she was gone respect me or she was gone have an issue. My dad taught me not to commit before you get ready. He tried to be serious with my mama and couldn't, ended up cheating on her with a few bitches and broke her heart. She was never the same after that. I don't know if Khadija noticed it, but I did. She stopped smiling as much, she didn't go out with her friends as much. She put her all into raising us. Not saying that it was a bad thing because it really wasn't, but it just wasn't her.

"Throw that ass back! Fuck you running for?" I asked smacking her ass.

Nothing about her was like Money. That's what I wanted when I decided to fuck her, but now that I was actually fucking her, I didn't want anything to do with her. Her arch was off, she couldn't ride it, and now she wasn't fucking me back, she was running, on top of the fact that her pussy was loose. I mean I ain't fall in, but it wasn't that super tight, monster grip my baby had.

Yeah, Money was my baby as bad as I hated to admit it fucking Money felt like home. Her pussy made me want to climb in that mother and just live there. I loved that she was super clean which made me comfortable with wanting her pretty clean-shaven pussy on my tongue constantly. Trina was cool and all, but she was so far away from Money it was ridiculous, and Money couldn't even tell. She was so busy trying to make sure I wasn't fucking nobody, but her that she hadn't realized she was in a league of her own.

"Put that ass up," I demanded smacking her ass again.

"You too deep!" she tossed over her shoulder.

I snatched my dick out of her, rushed over to the toilet and snatched the condom off my dick. After I pissed, I came back out to the main part of the hotel room. Trina was stretched out across the bed in the same spot her ass was in when I pulled my dick out of her.

"Come back to bed," she moaned looking over at me.

It was crazy that her body was on point, but that was the extent of what she had going on for herself.

"Nah, I actually got some shit to do, get dressed, I'll drive you home," I told her stepping into my jeans.

"Damn, it's like that? You didn't even cum," she pointed out. "It's okay, I'll call an UBER and …"

"Yo, I ain't got time to be going back and forth. Get ready to go and be in that car when I'm there," I replied, not waiting any time before I redressed.

I pulled up to Trina's apartment and parked before I walked her up to her door. I wasn't trying to intentionally make her feel like shit, so I went out of my way by walking her to the door instead of just dropping her off and leaving.

"You want to come in? I can cook you something or—"

"Trina, I fuck with you, but we gotta cool out. I told you I was fucking with somebody—"

"The crazy bitch from the mall?" she asked with a wild expression.

"Don't call her a bitch, but yeah," I nodded.

"So, you rather deal with her crazy pop-ups and talking crazy to people?" she asked crossing her arms over her chest.

"It doesn't matter, yo. You cool and like I said I fuck with you," I shrugged.

"You fuck with me, but basically you done fucking me?" she asked understanding what I was saying perfectly.

"You smart shorty," I said with a slight laugh.

"Not smart enough," I heard from behind me.

I closed my eyes briefly before I turned around to see Money standing behind me.

"What are you doing here?" I asked looking over her outfit.

"Making good on my promise to kill yo little girlfriend," she said nonchalantly.

"You like sounding crazy, don't you?" I asked.

I couldn't help but smile seeing her dressed in all black with her gun on the holster on her hip.

"I don't have to sound crazy, I'm a looney toon," she replied.

"You out here dressed like the black Tomb Raider, even got yo hair braided and shit," I laughed.

"Can y'all take y'all little crazy show somewhere else?" Trina asked rolling her eyes before unlocking her apartment and heading inside quickly.

"She lucky I don't make you fuck me outside her door. Stupid bitch," Money snapped as she kicked Trina's door with her foot.

"Can I ride with you?" I asked her pushing against her.

"No, but you can meet me at my house and dick me down there," she grinned devilishly.

"Bet," I nodded and headed over to her house.

Three hours later and Money still hadn't made it home. I called her phone and sent countless text messages before I realized she was trying to be funny. I went home only to find her car parked outside my mama's house.

"That's fucked up how you dissed me yo," I told her once I walked in.

"What you mean?" she asked with a wide grin.

"Aight, I guess maybe I deserved that shit," I shrugged.

"Oh, nah, I'm just getting started," she told me leaving out the house.

* * *

"Aight, fellas keep yo head on a swivel. We can't afford to mess this up," I told Saint and Kidd as we made our way through the door.

Our goal tonight was to take out another debtor. The only issue with this nigga was, he lived way out the way, close to an hour away. If niggas would just pay the shit they owed, niggas like me would have to find another way to get money. Speaking of Money, since she wasn't talking to me through text, by phone call, hell not even on social media, making me want to strangle the shit out her pretty ass. I was letting her run for now, but when I had some free time, I was putting her pretty pussy on my tongue.

I shook off thoughts of Money that constantly crept into the corners of my mind and focused on the task at hand. We crept into the nigga's two-story condo, it wasn't as old as it appeared on the outside. The inside was decorated in black and blue shit which was cool. This was something I wanted one day, something in the cut, something nobody really knew about.

"I'ma give y'all bitches until the count of ten to put the guns down and get the fuck out my shit," a deep voice spoke from a few feet away.

"Or you can eat bullets and we take yo shit," a female's voice spat.

From where I was standing, it was no way I could take a shot and make it, I had to get closer. We crept in closer to get a better view, but Mr. Greg Burton, the man that owed Ace more than fifty thousand dollars was actually shooting back and holding his own against a group of women.

I stepped out of the stairwell and took the kill shot, hitting him square in the middle of his head.

"What the fuck?" Money asked snatching the mask from her face.

"If anything, I should be the one snapping. Fuck you doing here?" I asked her.

"Minding my damn business," she sassed brushing past me to the safe in the wall.

"Nah, you ain't about to get off that fucking easily yo," I told her snatching her arm off the safe.

"You think it's cool to be out here playing cops and robbers and shit?" Saint asked Sinna who was ignoring him as she walked around in her mask.

"What the fuck is up with you?" I asked Money making her focus on me.

"Why it matter to you? I'm just another hoe you fucked right?" she asked staring into my eyes.

"I'm sorry for the shit I said. I shouldn't have said that shit to you and I'm sorry aight?" I told her.

"No, it ain't alright and I don't know when it ever will be. That shit you said really hurt my feelings and I'm not ready to let go of it yet," she said.

"You seem pretty ready to let go the other day when you were outside of ole girl's house," I reminded her.

"Khalifa why are you suddenly everywhere I am?" she asked rolling her eyes.

"I'm handling my business, you the one out here and can't shoot. After this, let me take you to the gun range so we can get some practice in. I mean you ain't gone listen, so I gotta find a way to keep you protected," I told her hanging my head.

"See was that so hard?" she asked rubbing my chin hair before her and Sinna went over to the safe.

"Where is Khadija?" Kidd asked making me snap my head up to see what they were going to say.

"She's down in the car—"

"Why the fuck would she be in the car? I barked.

"You said don't involve her in my shit, and technically she ain't involved, she's just playing lookout. She doesn't come in, and she doesn't do anything that we're doing," Money explained.

"You want me to fuck you up." I told her pointing a finger in her face.

"So, what you want her to do? Sit at home and twirl her fingers?" Sinna asked propping her hand on her hips.

"Saint get yo girl. Money yo ass don't listen, but I'ma fix you. Hurry up so we can get the fuck out of here," I replied.

"I can't wait for you to spank me later, I been such a bad girl," Money moaned in my ear before she kissed it, sending shivers through me.

"And daddy definitely about to punish yo ass," I promised licking my lips.

SINNA

SINNA

"Sinna, call me back, I need you to get Justyce for me," Simone's voice played over my voicemail.

It had been more than a month since I talked to my sister, but I couldn't help but hear the seriousness in her voice. I missed her call because I was in class, but now she wasn't answering the phone. Well actually it was going straight to voicemail and it was bothering me.

"Still straight to voicemail?" Saint asked as he came back into the room.

We were in his apartment, I was stretched across his bed with all my books spread out in front of me. He put the Cookout bag on the bed and rubbed my knee. After that bull-shit that happened in the mall with him and his new little bitch, we just decided not to talk about it. He wanted to have a clear conscience while he fucked other people, I hated it, but what was the alternative? Not fuck with him at all? That wasn't an option.

"Don't stress yo self out, you know how yo sister get down," he replied.

"What?" I asked with an attitude.

Yeah, Simone had her faults, but she was my fucking sister, and wrong or not she was all I had. So, the only motherfucka that could talk shit about her was me. I knew he didn't mean nothing by his statement, but it felt like everything he did or said I had an issue with.

"I'm just saying, you know she ain't the most reliable and shit," he shrugged.

"Nah, I don't care. That's my fucking sister and something is wrong with her. I gotta look out for her," I replied picking up my books and shit.

"So, you get in your feelings about me telling the truth?" he asked with a smirk.

"I should smack that smirk off yo fucking face!" I barked as I stood up.

"You can try," he said pulling his food out of the bag.

"I'm ready to go home," I said tossing my bookbag on my back.

"Aight, eat this shit I just bought and then I'll take you," he told me no longer paying attention to me and focusing on ESPN that was now on the TV.

"No, I'm ready to go home now," I told him, folding my arms across my chest.

"Then you can get to that motherfucka however you want, but I ain't leaving out until after I eat," he shrugged, shoving French fries in his mouth.

"I swear you can be so fucking childish," I growled.

"Says the girl who mad cause I called her hoe sister, a hoe," he said with a mouth full of food.

"Just stop fucking talking to me," I hissed.

"Sayless," he replied biting into his burger without looking at me.

An hour later I was still at his house, only now I was waiting for an UBER while he thought I was just sitting over here pouting. Once I knew my UBER was outside, I waited until he wasn't paying me any attention and I walked out, hopped in my UBER, and left his childish ass.

* * *

I was falling in love and I knew it.

After leaving Saint's apartment like an escapee, he was calling my phone back to back.

"What?" I hissed.

"Where you at?" he asked yelling into the phone.

"In my damn skin! What you want?" I asked.

"So, that's what we do now? You just up and leave and don't say shit? You heard me say I was gone take yo ass home yo," he groaned.

I knew just by the sound of his voice he was standing beside the recliner he loved to sit in while he watched TV, phone pressed against his ear as he talked to me or yelled at me rather. He was shaking his head, clenching his fists open and closed and once he got really upset and was ready to blow his top, he'd start pacing the floor. When he paced the floor, I knew he was going to demolish my pussy.

Saint was confident and cocky as hell. I don't know who told the nigga he had a big dick and could knock the dust off some pussy, but that nigga knew, and it was no turning back now. He made me weak, I was addicted to the way he said my name while he was deep inside me. Being so involved with him was dangerous, it wasn't healthy at all, it was destroying me, it was driving me completely insane.

Saint could fuck me and make me cum three or four times before even nutting once. He ate pussy like he was starving and not only was pussy the last meal on earth, it was his favorite. I knew I wasn't the only bitch he was fucking, but he said I was important and initially that had been enough. Now, that I was spending more time with him I was losing control of all forms of sense I thought I had.

I couldn't keep stressing myself out about him though because I needed to lay eyes on my sister and my nephew.

"I told you I needed to try to find my sister and my nephew," I replied.

"Okay, and I could have taken you to go do that," he replied.

"Well, I'll call you in a couple of hours," I told him before I hung up the phone.

Two hours later, Money and I were knocking on Dirty's door.

"What's up?" he asked coming to the door eating an apple.

"Where are Simone and Justyce?" I asked as soon as he opened the door.

"Hell, if I know?" he shrugged as he glanced at Money.

"What up Money, you looking good baby," he flirted with her.

"Nigga, where the hell is Simone and y'all's son? Ain't body got time to be playing with you," Money told him.

"Look, I don't know what the hell Simone told you, but she left out of here ranting and raving about how I won't shit, and I won't gone ever be shit. She told me she was going to stay with you," he said looking at me.

"Me? I live with Money, how she gone come live with me? I asked him.

"Ask her," he shrugged.

"Maybe I could if her phone wasn't going straight to voicemail," I told him raising my eyebrows.

"What you want me to do about it? Hunt her crazy ass down and turn her phone on for her?" he asked with a frown.

"No, I want yo dumb ass to act like the woman you've been living with the past few months and your fucking son are missing, and you actually give a fuck!" I yelled at him.

"Sinna, last time I saw yo sister she had her back to me as she climbed inside a red pick-up out there in the parking lot. I asked her repeatedly to leave Justyce, but she wouldn't leave him with me. That was almost a month ago." he shrugged.

"Did she say where she was going?" I pressed him again.

"I told you no already. If I hear from her then I'll tell her to call you," he shrugged putting the coffee cup to his crusty, peeling lips.

"Where Khadija?" he asked.

The fact that his dumb ass actually expected an answer was funny.

We went around the city to her so-called friends' houses looking for my sister before finally, we ended up at the police station where I filed a police report. Later that night I was laying on Saint's chest playing with his chest hair while I listened to his heart beating.

"What you thinking about over there?" he asked pulling at my dreads playfully.

"This shit with my sister," I replied.

"She's going to be fine, her and lil man," he told me and kissed my jaw.

"Is that all that's bothering you?" he asked.

I felt his eyes on me and I knew if I didn't speak up now, that I probably never would.

"What are we doing?" I blurted out.

"What you mean?" he asked moving me off his chest to the side of his body as he stared at me intently.

"I mean what are we doing? You said you don't want to have a relationship with me, but I don't know where to go with that information. I mean if we aren't building to that, then what are we doing?" I asked him, looking into his handsome face.

"This whole no title shit is really bugging you I see," he said kissing my lips.

"It's messy. I mean you ain't my nigga, but you act like you're single and I'm stuck watching you and I hate it," I replied.

"Let's make it easy for you. I already told you I don't want nobody else," he replied.

"But you're not my boyfriend?"

"Why does the label mean so much? Husbands cheat on their wives all the time. That label ain't gone stop a man from fucking someone else if that's why they want to do." he shrugged.

"You claim you just out here "handling your business" but bitches flock to you. I really don't know if I can trust you," I told him.

"Let's worry about tomorrow when it comes, so stop over analyzing baby. Come ride yo dick and let me put you to sleep," he told me.

Later that night when I dozed off, I was wrapped in Saint's arms. When I opened my eyes the next morning, I was alone. I sat up in the bed and glanced at the sunlight shining in through the window. It had to be at least 9 in the morning. I yelled into the pillow beside me because I'd spilled my guts to him about how I felt and now he was running away.

"Damnnnnn!" I yelled into the pillow again.

I stood out of the bed and walked over to the bathroom. After taking care of my hygiene I wrapped a towel around me and brushed my teeth. I walked into the living room to make sure the front door was locked. And as soon as I walked into the living room, I saw a vase with white flowers on the table and a cardboard rectangular box on the couch. I sat down on the couch and looked at the box.

It was a MacBook!

I needed a computer so bad and here it was in my hands. I looked down at the card on the table and picked it up. I opened the card and smiled to see a couple holding hands on the card. The card read "Thinking of you" on the front. I turned to the inside of the card and could stop smiling.

"I know you didn't ask for a laptop, but you gotta finish school and you need it. I respect ya hustle, ma and I'm here for you. Don't sweat the

title, know that what matters is my heart and as far as I'm concerned it's yours."

I tore open the laptop box with a big ass grin on my face.

* * *

"Alright, I'm here. What did you need to talk to me about?" I asked Money as I walked into her room the next day.

"I been thinking about some shit the past few days. I think I got away to put an end to our money problems," she said with a grin.

We didn't really have money problems though. Our rent was paid three months in advance and we paid all our other bills off top without any help from anyone else. It seemed like it didn't matter what was going on with our finances, Money was constantly on the next get rich quick scheme.

"Money, we're good. We don't have to worry about money, right now," I told her.

"You think three months is enough time to find another job and have enough money to pay rent again?" she asked raising an eyebrow.

"What do you want me to do?" I asked her skeptically.

"Really, you'll just be my lookout. Nothing more," she said raising her hand.

"Your lookout? What is it that you're doing?" I asked her squinting at her.

"Sinna, please. If I tell you, then you'll try to talk me out of it, and you can't. I need this," she told me.

"Money, you don't *have* to, you *want* to. It's a difference," I told her.

"You think I'm talking about killing Khalifa's little bitch? Girl, that bitch is the least of my worries. A little birdie told me that it's a nigga that got a large amount of cash in a building not too far from here," she replied.

"How much?" I asked watching her.

"Less than a hundred, but more than fifty." she smiled.

"Thousand?" I asked with wide eyes.

"I said the same shit. Come on, we gotta dress like the waitresses so we can get close to him.

"All I'm doing is being a lookout," I reminded her.

"Girl, after we hit this lick, we gone be straight," she said dancing playfully.

The small hole in the wall club, was standing room only. Niggas were grabbing ass, women were shaking ass and I was more than ready to go home. I glanced at Money and she smiled and nodded her head. I rolled my eyes but stuck to the plan and headed to the back of the shack that probably should have been condemned years ago, especially since it was really a house that someone converted into a piece of shit club.

Finally, reaching the office area, I danced, flirted, and shook my ass for a couple of tips as I stood outside of the waiting area waiting on some nigga we'd never seen before named Ty to come unlock the door for us.

"Sorry to keep y'all pretty ladies waiting so long," Ty said coming towards us as he juggled the key in the lock.

I stood beside him and Money stood behind me waiting for him to open the door. He opened the door and we all walked into the dimly lit office. He walked around the desk to the safe. He was only supposed to hand us a stack of money that was already broken up, but we didn't want that little change we wanted all the shit.

"Empty it," Money told him, snatching the small black gun from her inner thigh.

"Y'all bitches making a big mistake! You don't even know how big of a fucking mistake you're making right now!" Ty yelled as she directed him to keep filling the bag.

Once we had all the money from the safe tightly packed in the small bookbag, we had we tied Ty to a chair.

"Yo, I'ma kill y'all bitches!" he growled.

"You gone kill us?" Money asked taunting him with a smile.

She sat on his lap and ground into him subtly before she wrapped her arms around his neck and kissed his forehead leaving her red lipstick planted at the top of his head.

"You can't fuck yo way out of this." Ty spat looking at me.

"You're right," she said before pushing the gun in his head and squeezing the trigger.

The security team went into action around us and I knew we needed to move quickly.

"Let's go!" I yelled to her as we raced out of the office.

"Aye! Hold up!" someone was yelling behind us.

I knew someone probably saw us running out of the office, but it was nothing I could do about it now. I couldn't go back in time and change the shit, so I put one foot in front of the other and tried to get out of the hole in the wall that had only one way in and one way out. People were screaming around us and fighting their way to get out of the small place. I turned around and locked eyes with a nigga that was locked and focused on me and Money.

"You see that nigga back there? He doesn't look like he playing!" I yelled just as gunfire erupted in the small space.

I could have sworn it was the nigga shooting at me, but the shots were actually being fired from in front of us, forcing the crowd to scatter.

"Take the bag and get to the car, I'll meet you—"

Her words were cut off by the nigga that was staring at us grabbing us both by our arms as we fought against him. He pushed us back in the office with Ty's dead body sending me screaming at the top of my lungs. The steel door slammed shut leaving us alone with Ty's dead body, I noticed the money bag wasn't even with us anymore.

"Where's the bag?" I asked her.

"He took it," she said dropping her shoulders and hitting the door with an open palm.

"Why are we in here? Why didn't he just kill us when he had the chance?" I asked Money as we looked around the room.

An hour later we were sitting on the floor of the steel door waiting to die. The door popped open unexpectedly and Saint and Khalifa were pushed into the room with guns to their backs.

"What are you doing here?" Saint asked me looking over my all back attire and then coming back up to my face.

I was so scared, I was terrified. I didn't know what else to do so I wrapped my arms around him and sobbed into his chest.

"You killed that nigga?" Khalifa asked Money, he looked like he was pissed as he put two and two together.

The empty safe, the dead nigga tied to a chair. It didn't take a rocket scientist to put two and two together and figure out we were caught trying to rob whoever owned this shit.

"You're just like your sister," a deep voice spoke once the door opened.

A tall and large body blocked the door, refusing entry or exit to anyone attempting to get by him.

"I'm just like my sister? Nigga, you don't know me!" Khalifa snapped.

"I tried to save her too, but you see biting the hand that feeds you doesn't get you anywhere," the voice spoke again.

"Fletch?" Khalifa asked tilting his head to the side.

"The one and only," he replied gruffly.

I still hadn't told Saint about him possibly being my father and now that he was standing in front of me my heart was pounding in my chest.

"It seems we have a problem, gentlemen. Your women have decided to touch things that don't belong to them. They emptied my safe," he growled, tossing the bag in the center of the floor. "You know how I feel about thieves," he replied.

"Maybe we should cut them some slack, they didn't get out with any of it—"

Khalifa's voice was cut off with a hand raise.

The room was eerily quiet as everyone focused their attention on me. I stepped around Saint as he grabbed for me, attempting to stop me from moving forward, but I couldn't help myself. Finally, I was standing arm's length away from him. The lighting in the room was the bare minimum, but through it, I could see a small hint of something familiar with him. I took the last step that made our feet touch and craned my neck to see into his face.

His eyes…we shared the same eyes.

"How y'all know each other?" Saint asked standing beside me.

"I think he's my dad." I whispered while still staring at him.

TO BE CONTINUED…

Thank you for reading! Please leave a review and tell me if you liked it or hated either way I want to hear from you!

Thank you for reading We Thuggin' part 1, the link to part 2 is on the next page. Feel free to leave a review good, bad or in between. To keep up with all things Taylor B please join my reading group on Facebook, Don't Bother me I'm Reading. You can also follow me on Instagram at Taylorb_theauthor.

Peace and Blessings,

Taylor B

ALSO BY TAYLOR B,

Luvin' A Carolina Menace

Sprung off a Hustler's Love

We Thuggin': Saint & Sinna's Story

We Thuggin' 2: Saint & Sinna's Story

We Thuggin' 3: Saint & Sinna's Story

We Thuggin' 4: Saint & Sinna's Story

Hood Love & Heartbreak

Donovon and Shadaye: Testing his gangsta, Trying her loyalty

Donovan and Shadaye 2: Testing his gangsta, Trying her loyalty

Donovon and Shadaye 3: Testing his gangsta, Trying her Loyalty

Hood Love and Heartbreak 2

Caught up with a Queen City Savage 1-3

Deuce and Trinity: In Love with a Real One

A Dope Boy Got me Faded 1-2

Loving a Sin City Menace

Falling for a Dirty South Dope Boy

Holidays with a Hood Boy

My Savage Gave to Me